SPECIAL WITCH OF THE FBI

SCHOOL OF NECESSARY MAGIC RAINE CAMPBELL™
BOOK 03

JUDITH BERENS   MARTHA CARR   MICHAEL ANDERLE

SPECIAL WITCH OF THE FBI TEAM

Thanks to our beta reading team

Mary Morris, Kelly O'Donnell, Larry Omans, and Chrisa Changala

Thanks to the JIT Readers

Diane L. Smith
Angel LaVey
Micky Cocker
Daniel Weigert
Misty Roa
Keith Verret
Larry Omans
Jeff Eaton

If we've missed anyone, please let us know!

Editor
The Skyhunter Editing Team

From Martha

To everyone who still believes in magic
and all the possibilities that holds.
To all the readers who make this
entire ride so much fun.
And to my son, Louie and so many wonderful friends who
remind me all the time of what
really matters and how wonderful
life can be in any given moment.

From Michael

To Family, Friends and
Those Who Love
To Read.
May We All Enjoy Grace
To Live The Life We Are
Called.

CHAPTER ONE

Raine practically jumped out of Agent Connor's car when they pulled to a stop in front of the school. She had enjoyed her time with Uncle Jerry, but she was excited to be back with her friends. Evie and Sara rushed forward and pulled her into a tight hug. Raine noticed Evie had some buttercream on her cheek.

"You've been back for an hour and you're already baking?" Raine laughed. "Did you have a good summer? I missed you guys."

"I've been back for three hours." Evie grinned and wiped the buttercream from her cheek. "I wanted to make cupcakes to celebrate having you guys back again. I found a recipe for the most amazing lemon meringue cupcakes. I haven't mastered the meringue on the top, so they're just lemon buttercream. They're so good, though!"

"I've already eaten two." Sara gave Raine a shameless look. "Did you do much over summer?"

"I hung out with Cameron and William for a week. That was cool. Uncle Jerry wasn't quite ready for me to go and stay with them, so they stayed in a hotel and we hung out together. I showed them all my favorite haunts. None of them compare to the kemana and here, though."

"We need to go to Bubble and Fizz tomorrow!" Sara picked up Raine's bag which Agent Connor had removed from the car. "Come on. I want every detail. Adrien and Philip are back and they're probably eating the cupcakes."

"Thanks for the ride, Agent Connor." Raine waved to him as she was pulled along by Sara. "I've told you everything."

"Oh, come on!" Evie nudged Raine. "You spent a week with Cameron."

Raine blushed. She had enjoyed spending that time with him, and William had really relaxed and found new confidence.

They headed inside and moved around the groups of students who had been dropped off and had begun to haul their luggage inside. Raine watched a particularly small freshman try to carry a suitcase almost as big as she was. Several others rushed to help her and greeted her as they lifted her suitcase and pointed to the front door. Adrien and Philip jogged down the stairs toward them. They greeted Raine with light hugs before the elf took her bags and carried them up the stairs.

"How was summer?" Philip glanced over his shoulder. "Did anything exciting happen?"

"It was peaceful." Raine smiled. "It was the break I needed."

"Cameron told us about the amazing froyo place you took him to." Philip held out his hand to take Raine's bag from Adrien and give him a break. "I did a lot of charity work. It was amazing. I got to really help people and saw firsthand the difference my efforts made."

"I put in plenty of training. After the…incident I wanted to really improve my combat magic and overall game." Adrien handed Philip the backpack. "I talked my grandmother into giving me some of her pastry recipes, though, Evie. I'll give them to you later."

Evie's face split into a brilliant grin. "Thank you. That's amazing."

The elf shrugged. "No worries."

"I traveled a little with my older sister. We went down to Mexico, and it was absolutely incredible." Sara hooked her arm through Raine's. "I've also started learning pastels and watercolors. They don't come as easily to me as acrylic and oil do, but I'm really enjoying experimenting. I find that I get a very different feel with them, and that means I put different emotions and focus into those projects."

"Wow, that sounds amazing." Adrien shifted the weight of Raine's bag. "I'm glad you have your art. You're really talented."

Sara walked a little taller and felt pride swell within her. She put far more work and practice into her art than she let on and it felt good to hear that it had all paid off.

Adrien and Philip paused at the doorway of the girls' room. They weren't really supposed to be there to begin with and they didn't want to push their luck too much. Raine left her bag to be unpacked later. She wanted to enjoy time with her friends first.

Cameron bounded down the hallway and Raine had barely stepped out of her room when she felt his strong arms wrap around her. She leaned into him and wound her arms around his neck to rest her head on his shoulder. The summer had felt long without him around and she was glad to have physical contact again.

Evie took the lead with William, who still tried to find his confidence with his new girlfriend. She pulled him close and kissed his cheek.

"I missed you." She ran her fingers through his hair. "Did you have a good summer?"

"I had the most amazing time with Cameron. The pack let me run with them one night. I had to stop after a while as they're much quicker than me, but I stargazed and felt a peace like I've never felt before." He smiled at Evie. "I missed you too. I know I'm bad at expressing stuff, but I missed the quiet moments we have together."

"Are there any of those cupcakes left?" Philip put his hands in his pockets and tried to hide the awkwardness he felt. "Your cupcakes are the best I've ever tasted, Evie."

"Evie baked cupcakes?" Cameron's ears pricked as he put his arm around Raine's waist. "Wait, you already baked cupcakes? I thought you got here like an hour before us?"

Evie shrugged and leaned against William.

"I love baking, and it seemed like a nice celebration to see everyone again."

"Well, it sounds like we have to find these cupcakes while there's still a chance." Adrien started down the hallway. "There are still some left, right?"

Evie and Sara laughed.

"I saved two each for everyone." Sara tucked her hands in her pockets. "They're really good. You're lucky I didn't sneak them away to eat all by myself."

"I think the real question here is whether there really is

a better way to celebrate our reunion than a batch of Evie's cupcakes." Philip looked back at the group. "Because I really can't think of anything."

"Brownies," William and Cameron said at the same time.

Everyone laughed.

"You're rubbing off on each other." Raine looked up at Cameron. "It's kind of adorable."

He wrinkled his nose as he didn't particularly enjoy being thought of as adorable.

"I guess I could bake some brownies…really nice gooey, chewy brownies." Evie shrugged and smirked. "Maybe."

"What do we need to bribe you with?" William squeezed her hand gently. "You know we'll do about anything for your baking."

She looked mischievous. "I'll give it some thought."

"We don't need a stealth spell to go down to the kemana now," Sarah said. "This means we need to go to Bubble and Fizz before classes start tomorrow."

"I liked the stealth spells." William smiled ruefully. "They added a bit of fun."

"It'll be nice to be able to go there freely, though." Evie hooked her arm around William's. "Do you want to share a pizza with me? No pineapple!"

"Sounds good." William thought for a moment. "Pepperoni and Parma ham?"

"Perfect." Evie looked at the others. "Are you guys going sweet or savory?"

They strolled across the grounds toward the cave and the kemana entrance.

"I'd love a banana split," said Cameron. "I haven't had one in years."

"Each to their own." Philip wrinkled his nose. "I think I need one of their sundaes. I'm not sure which flavor yet."

"Oh yes! I swear I've dreamt of their sundaes." Raine

leaned into Cameron. "I want something tart and sweet—lime and dark chocolate, maybe."

"You know, that might make a really good cupcake flavor, or maybe some mini tarts." Evie chewed her bottom lip as she tried to formulate the recipe. "I think tarts would work better if you used a thick chocolate ganache with lime rind, maybe?"

"Will I lose you to the kitchen?" William smiled at her. "You have a glow about you when you think about new recipes."

"You could always come and join me." Evie nudged him gently. "I'm sure the pixies would be happy to help teach you."

"I just might." William stepped back and waited for the others. "I'm open to learning new things."

Evie grinned and looked forward to sharing her passion with him. He had made great improvements with his potions and she had high hopes for his skills as a baker.

The group made their way into the kemana without a stealth spell for the first time. Raine felt a little weird as she strolled casually down the stairs without the slight weight of the spell. She looked around at the underground city and drank in the beautiful array of colors and the slight tingle of magic as they stepped into the city proper.

Cameron breathed deeply and smiled. The kemana had come to have strong positive associations for him. He took in the scents of magic, life, and a wide variety of different foods. A feeling of warm happiness filled him, and he held Raine a little closer. They had been through so much during the last year and he couldn't wait to see where this new semester took them.

Philip and Sara led the way through the crowds of witches bartering over crystals and Kilomea whispering something that sounded philosophical to Raine's ear. A pair of shifters with amber eyes strutted down the middle of the walkway toward them. Cameron rolled his eyes. They looked to be relatively new and had the insecurity that came with that. He came from a long line of shifters and didn't feel the need to remind everyone what he was. These shifters were older than him but were probably only second generation. Their families would have been changed by the dark wizard families and he hoped they grew to become comfortable in their own skin. Being a shifter was something he took great pride in.

They meandered their way through the streets that overflowed with shops and life and looked casually in windows. Evie paused at a shop selling potted plants.

"Oh! Look, there are some that can't be killed." She looked at Raine. "We could get one for our room."

"The blue one is pretty." Sara pointed at the small plant with delicate blue flowers. "That could fit on our window sill too."

"We'll get it on the way back." Raine turned toward the bookshop where Bubble and Fizz was. "I'd feel a bit weird having a plant on the table while we ate."

"Oh, ouch, maybe not." Evie pointed at the price tag. "I misread it. I thought it had fewer zeros."

Raine raised an eyebrow.

"People must really love unkillable plants." She took a few steps down the walkway. "Should we head straight to Bubble and Fizz now?"

"I think so. I'm dying for my pizza." William glanced at

the others. "But I'll live if someone wants to keep window shopping."

"No, we're good." Philip smiled. "I'm definitely window-shopped out."

"Agreed." Sara walked down the walkway. "And there will be other cool little things for our room."

They continued to the bookshop and Adrien walked immediately to the book that would open the entrance into Bubble and Fizz. They descended the stairs and were happy to find the cafe bursting to the brim. Raine had hoped they found plenty of business to keep them going. She didn't want to lose their little hangout.

The fairy led them to the last available booth where a bowl of mixed M&Ms waited for them. Sara had barely sat down when she took a handful.

"Dude, they have every flavor." She put another two in her mouth. "There's chocolate, crispy, mint, caramel—they're so good."

Raine took a few and offered them to Cameron. They picked at the M&Ms while Adrien decided what he wanted to order. He settled on a decadent triple chocolate and mint sundae. Sara scooted a little closer to him.

"Talk to me."

The elf looked at her with a raised eyebrow. "I'm sorry?"

"You've been quiet. So, talk to me."

Adrien laughed. "I haven't had anything to say. I'm fine."

Sara narrowed her eyes. "Are you sure?"

"One hundred percent."

She continued to look at him for a long moment before she finally smiled and let him be.

"You know, I'm actually looking forward to classes starting." Philip took another few M&Ms. "I think we'll start digging into the really cool stuff this year."

"Don't forget the extra dark magic classes we have to take." Raine thanked the fairy for her sundae. "It'll be a really busy year."

"They'll be awesome, though." Sara took a mouthful. "Do we get extra credit for those classes?"

"You know, I didn't ask." Evie took a slice of her and William's pizza. "I'm okay if we don't. I think the classes will be awesome."

"Professor Powell can be scary." William bit into his pizza. "He's really talented, though. We'll be in a great position to kick ass thanks to him."

"We've done a pretty good job of that so far." Philip grinned. "We saved those druids, don't forget."

He carefully didn't mention Adrien's kidnapping as he didn't want to make the elf feel bad.

"True. I'll go into the FBI with Raine, though, so the better at ass-kicking I am, the more likely they are to take me." William finished his first slice. "We'll make the agency proud and show them how well magicals and humans can work together."

"We'll make a big difference." Philip raised his root beer. "To the bright future ahead of us all."

CHAPTER THREE

Philip was walking to dinner when the headmistress stopped him in the hallway.

"You will be pleased to hear that politics classes will begin this semester as an elective. We have found a suitable teacher, and there is room in your schedule to take it if you wish to do so." The headmistress put her hands behind her back. "I believe you made the right call in pushing for this."

"Thank you. I can't wait to begin those classes." Philip nodded his head. "I really appreciate your efforts, but I must get to dinner."

"Of course." The headmistress turned away. "Enjoy."

Philip couldn't keep the smile off his face. He had studied global and national politics over the summer and couldn't wait to start on those classes. He was particularly interested in the future integration of magicals and humans. There was a lot of room there to bring the two groups together.

"You look cheerful. Did something good happen?"

William waited for Philip at the bottom of the stairs. "Did you figure out a new business scheme?"

The wizard laughed. "Not yet. The headmistress told me politics classes will be an elective this year, though. It'll be a great start to my political career."

"You're definitely going into politics, then?" the half-Ifrit walked toward the dining hall. "You made the decision?"

"Yeah. All that charity work showed me that the best way I can make a positive change is through politics." Philip shrugged. "Business has a lot of potential, and I will have to run a small business to fund my political career. My focus is to bring about real change, though."

William respected that. He had no interest in politics himself, but he knew Philip would make a good politician.

A group of freshmen was absolutely delighted when their food appeared seemingly out of nowhere on the white plates in front of them. It was their first dinner at the school and everything was wonderfully new.

Raine had settled at their usual table with Sara and the others. Cameron played his fingers over hers and smiled gently while Adrien and Sara tried to figure out what bribe was best to get Evie to bake brownies. William and Philip joined them, and the pixies began putting their food out.

As it always did, the food appeared from thin air. The rich aroma of lasagna with a side of green vegetables filled the air. Raine didn't wait on ceremony. It smelled far too good to delay. She wasn't disappointed. It was the best lasagna she'd ever tasted with the meat perfectly balanced with creamy cheeses.

"Did you see the politics classes on the list of electives?" Evie looked at Philip. "That was your doing, right?"

"Yeah. I'm signing up after dinner." Philip took a mouthful of his lasagna. "Do you know which electives you're taking this year?"

"I'll do politics with you." Cameron pushed the green beans away from his lasagna so they didn't contaminate the good food. "Then, I'll do military history, social history, and magical languages."

"Huh. I didn't know shifters got an extra elective." Sara picked at her cabbage. "I'll do art history and magical languages."

"It's because we're awesome." Cameron grinned. "We do more sports too."

"I've chosen magical languages and I haven't decided on my second one yet." Raine took another mouthful of her lasagna. "Military history sounds cool, but I feel like anatomy and physiology might be really useful too."

"Come and join me in military history." Cameron nudged her with his shoulder. "We can hang out and do our homework together."

Raine had to admit she liked the idea of an excuse to spend more time with Cameron. She was sure military history would have some benefits to her FBI plans too.

The pixies treated the students to a chocolate pie with extra whipped cream for dessert.

"I really don't know how I'll survive in college." Philip stood up "There's no way I can make food anywhere near this good."

"And I don't think student accommodations are usually great for cooking and baking." Raine finished her water.

"They usually live on toast and whatever can be microwaved, I think."

Everyone laughed.

"Not me." Evie stood up. "I'll make sure I can bake and cook proper meals."

"Aren't you going to culinary school?" Sara grinned at her. "It'd be weird if they didn't let culinary students cook."

"That's very true!" Evie laughed. "I don't know why I didn't think of that."

A group of juniors came over to their table.

"Sara, hey. Can we talk a minute?" A tall red-headed girl smiled at Sara. "We're in art club with you."

"Sure." Sara smiled, stood, and walked toward them. "What's up?" She followed them out of the dining hall to a quiet corner near the front door.

"We're putting on a mixed media art show." The redhead Sara remembered was called Isabelle folded her arms. "We'd love for you to put some pieces in."

Sara's eyes went big. She reeled with excitement. "Wow. I'd love to. Any particular media? How many pieces? Is there a theme?"

Isabelle grinned. "The theme is dark and stormy. Four pieces, and whatever media you're happiest with."

"What's the deadline?"

"Just over a month from now."

"Okay, I can do one oil and three acrylics in that time." Sara grinned like the Cheshire Cat. "Thank you so much for thinking of me."

"You're incredibly talented. We're honored to have you there with us." Isabelle stepped away. "See you in art club."

Sara bounced back to her friends and felt on top of the

world. Her art meant a lot to her, and she was so honored to have other people enjoy what she produced.

"What was that about?" Adrien scooted over to make room for Sara at the table once more. "You look like it went well."

"They invited me to be part of their art show." She felt as though she would burst with joy. "The theme is dark and stormy. I have a month to produce four pieces, which will be a little tight, but I know I can do it. Guys, I'm so excited!"

Evie stood and gave her a tight hug.

"We're so proud of you!" She squeezed Sara's shoulder. "I'm so happy to see your hard work paying off."

"That's an incredible achievement." Raine grinned at Sara. "Congratulations. You deserve so much success."

CHAPTER FOUR

"Today, we'll work on forming elemental walls." Professor Powell lifted his wand and formed a small wall of fire around the desk. "They are very useful spells, both defensively and offensively. Each of you will find that one or two elements come more easily than the others. This is natural and normal. I recommend you put the work in to master all of them, though."

He had spent the week before the students returned relaxing with Mara and creating a suitable lesson plan. He had agreed to give Raine and her friends extra lessons, something decided between himself, Agent Connor, and Mara. Raine showed strong inclinations toward her future as an FBI agent, and they wanted to make sure she could get herself out of the trouble she got into.

"You will begin with air. Push your magic into a clear wall shape while speaking the word *murus* clearly." He looked at the students before him. "Work in pairs. One will form the wall and the other will throw fireballs or some other projectile at it. Once you've mastered the wall around yourself, you can form it around your partner. Then next week, you'll learn how to push that wall into an assault." He smiled. "That will be a good test of your shields."

Someone in the front groaned and Xander held back his smirk. He was aware of some of the students' views of shields. They were necessary, though, and provided a solid foundation for more difficult workings.

Raine had done some reading on elemental walls but she didn't feel entirely confident. Fire and earth felt more natural to her, but water was her weakest.

"You do the wall first. I'll form projectiles." Evie turned to face Raine. "You can do this. Air is very calm and needs a little coaxing."

Raine took a slow, calming breath and tried to empty her mind. Her magic flowed quite well now. It still felt sluggish at times, but it moved into her wand without too much nudging. She began to feel out the image of the air wall in her mind and her magic locked up. A sigh formed on her lips, but she held it in. She wouldn't let her frustration rise.

The image of a solid wall of air finally came to her and she poked at her magic until it loosened up and began to move again. It was a slow process. The sound of projectiles pinging off other people's walls echoed around her, but she didn't let it get to her. She had made good progress and that was what really mattered.

When her magic moved well again, she pushed it into the image of a solid wall of air as she said *murus* clearly. Her magic sprang up into a short wall. It barely reached her knee, but it was better than she had expected. Evie began throwing small balls of earth at it and they disintegrated upon impact.

"That was great. Well done!" Evie grinned at Raine. "You're doing amazingly well."

William fought with his magic again. His Ifrit fire was easy to access and work with, but his other magic took a lot more wrangling. Air was one he could pull forward, but it took patience and focus. Adrien squeezed his shoulder and gave him a gentle smile.

"Don't fight with air. Allow it to flow through your fingers."

William focused on relaxing his body and he felt the air magic begin to trickle through. His Ifrit fire died down and finally, he could see how he would do this. He exhaled slowly and whispered the word on his next breath. The wall exploded up in front of him and stretched almost to the ceiling.

Adrien threw a series of throwing knives at it. Each dropped uselessly to the ground when it hit the wall.

"Well done, William." Professor Powell grinned at him. "That is the best example I've seen from a first try in a long time."

William felt his cheeks heat as everyone turned to look at him. He allowed the wall to fall and looked down at his desk. Whispering spread around the room but Adrien refused to let him think about that.

"My turn. Do you have a projectile in mind?"

"I think I can do small balls of earth. Evie taught me how."

Adrien nodded and rolled his shoulders before he

summoned the magic. It was almost instinctual to him. His parents had taught him combat from a young age and defensive and offensive magic came relatively easily to him thanks to that.

The wall of air burst up in front of the elf and William used a flick of energy to send the first earth projectile at him. To his surprise, it went through Adrien's wall and tapped his chest. The elf frowned and felt the wall flicker. He pulled on his magic and forced himself to focus. The next projectile dropped to the ground and William relaxed a little. He was used to Adrien making light work of the spells. Seeing him falter made him nervous and concerned.

Adrien had struggled with every form of wall they had gone through in the class. William took him to one side afterward.

"What's wrong?" Adrien looked away and thrust his hands into his pockets.

"I'm ashamed to have been kidnapped. It shouldn't have happened."

William rolled his eyes. "Stop letting your ego screw up your grade. No one's perfect. I bet Professor Powell has been caught out a few times, and I heard the headmistress was trapped in the World in Between for four years. They're both scary talented."

Adrien smiled and relaxed. "Yeah, okay, when you put it like that."

"Seriously." William gave the elf a very stern look.

"Move on. I understand that it was traumatic and embarrassing, but you can't let it consume you. You kick ass."

Adrien nodded and took his friend's words to heart. He knew he was being ridiculous and he couldn't afford to let his grades slip. His parents would never forgive him if he dropped below straight A's.

CHAPTER FIVE

Raine took her time walking back from the stables and stopped when she saw something odd. A group of freshmen sat on the grass and enjoyed the warm early evening. The stars began to bloom in the increasingly dark sky overhead. A form caught in the shadows stalked along the rise heading toward the back of the main school building. Raine frowned and peered more closely. It looked distinctly canine but too lean to be a shifter and it seemed reluctant to come any closer. The freshmen paused their conversation and looked at the form that had now paused and stared directly at them.

"Is that a dog?"

"I think so."

"Does that mean I can have a pet dog? Or is that a senior thing?"

"It's a school thing. You can't keep a dog in your dorm room."

Raine knew that there was a very strict no pets for students rule on the school grounds. The horses were an entirely separate thing. She walked toward the rise to see if the light perhaps played tricks or if there really was something there.

The shadowy form slipped away into the rising darkness. Raine retrieved the small flashlight she always carried when she knew she'd return to the school in the dark. She shone it on the grass where she was sure the form had been and was ready to shrug it off as a weird shadow when she saw the soft outline of a large paw print.

Leaning down, Raine looked more closely. It was definitely canine. The pads and claws were distinct when she knew where to look. Shining her torch in the direction the shadow had gone she looked for more pawprints. There were none.

She sighed and checked her watch. The library would be open for two more hours. Whatever had made those pawprints would bug her. She had potions and portals homework, but they weren't too urgent. Perhaps Librarian Decker would be able to tell her what it was. He enjoyed sharing little bits about the school and its history.

"I know that look." Librarian Decker smiled and rocked back on his heels. "You've heard or seen something and you need to find out what it is."

Raine laughed. The gnome knew her so well at this point.

"I saw something weird. It looked like a big black dog." Raine folded her arms. "I even found a pawprint. Only one, though."

A deep crease formed between his eyebrows. "No pets are allowed on the grounds. Horace has his dog, but it's not a big black one." He turned to Joe. "Have you heard anything about a big black dog on the grounds?"

"No, but there are many myths around them." Joe pointed toward the fairy mythology section of the library. "That'll be a good starting point if you're looking."

"This isn't a myth. Raine found a pawprint."

"A physical one." She smirked. "Not a mythological one."

Joe laughed. "You know better than to assume those myths are simply myths, Miss Campbell."

Raine laughed and shook her head before she looked at that section of the library. She really needed to do her homework, but it would niggle at her. Maybe if she set herself a time limit and only investigated the possibilities for half an hour. Nodding to herself, she decided that was perfectly reasonable.

Once she approached the shelves, she saw a great deal had been written on black dogs throughout the ages. There were many myths about them, some tied to very small areas. Raine sat down at her preferred table and began to read in earnest.

A good number of the myths seemed to come from Britain. There were a few black dog myths surrounding small villages. What she noticed was that in each of these, the animal related to death. Some had it as an omen of death coming soon, and others that death had just taken someone.

Raine pursed her lips. She didn't like the idea that a death omen wandered the school grounds. It didn't sit right with her. Not because she thought someone would die, but because she didn't think such things existed. That meant either someone was screwing with people and trying to scare them, or it meant something entirely different.

Raine checked the time and realized she only had ten minutes left before she was supposed to start her homework. She looked longingly at the shelves that contained the black dog myths and sighed. Her homework was far more important than digging into something that likely meant nothing at all. Still, she would mention it to the headmistress in case it was something they should be concerned about.

The homework was relatively easy, thankfully. She settled into the routine of looking through the relevant books and taking notes so she could write her essay up later. Everything came together far quicker than she had expected. That left her with plenty of time to head to the headmistress's office.

It was late at night but sometimes, Ms. Berens worked in her office after dinner. Raine hoped it was one of those instances. She didn't really want to take it to her before breakfast the next morning.

A soft light could be seen from beneath the office door and hushed voices came from within. Raine knocked and waited. She began to feel as though she was bothering them over nothing, but she'd rather know she'd done everything she could if it did turn out to be something serious.

The headmistress opened the door with a small, tired smile.

"I was about to leave." She stepped back. "Come in."

Professor Powell had made himself comfortable in a high-backed armchair and was reading an old book. He glanced up at Raine before he returned to reading.

"What can we help you with tonight?" The headmistress tucked a piece of hair behind her ear. "It is late."

"I saw a black dog on the grounds earlier." Raine stood a little straighter. "I found a physical pawprint that showed it wasn't a trick of the light."

"Thank you, Miss Campbell, we'll look into it." Professor Powell stood and placed his book on the desk. "I suggest you go to bed."

Raine itched to ask questions and find out what they thought it might be. The stern expression on both teachers' faces made her bite the inside of her cheek and stay quiet.

She turned and left, feeling somehow even less satisfied than she had before.

CHAPTER SIX

Xander and Mara shared a look—one that had developed from decades of familiarity and an uncomfortable number of incidents much like this one. They left the office and made sure to lock it behind them.

The headmistress led the way through the school and out into the darkness where the shadows seemed deeper. Xander cast a stealth spell over them to prevent the students from seeing what they were doing. She wasted no time but rushed to the vault door. It was a hidden place that looked like nothing more than an old, forgotten door into the basement. They had worked hard to make it look that way.

Xander stood guard and watched for intruders or errant students while Mara fumbled with her keys. The spell to unlock it came quickly to her lips. She hurried through it and almost skipped over consonants in her desire to prove her fears unfounded. Mara flung the door open and they ran down the old concrete steps into the dull darkness.

Light blossomed around them and revealed a second, more substantial door. Xander and Mara whispered the required words to move through the wards and open this. They ran into the well-lit space with forest-green marble floors and neat shelves carved from old hardwoods.

Turner Underwood had made sure that every small detail within his mansion was perfect. To an outsider, the shelves would have looked mismatched with redwood butted against mahogany and cedar beneath ash. They wouldn't realize that each wood had been chosen to house a particular type of artifact. The woods adhered to the wards and magics with slightly different resonances, which then affected how they reacted to the artifacts.

The old retired Fixer had left them in place, just as he had at his mansion in Washington, securely stored away for safekeeping. It was part of the arrangement with the government when opening the school.

After what happened to the old vault in Chicago when it was destroyed, and the artifacts scattered, he decided it was best to divide them up in different locations, hidden away. The new Fixer, Correk was given a map long ago of where everything was stored and their different properties.

Xander didn't worry about any of that as he ran across the marble and his shoes slipped on the smooth stone. He grabbed onto the edge of a titanium-edged shelf and used it to pull himself around to the farthest corner. There, his heart threatened to stop in his chest.

"It's gone, isn't it?" Mara joined him a few seconds later. "How?"

Xander shook his head and looked around for any signs of tampering. The wards had been in place. There were layers of them surrounding the vault itself, the doors, and the shelves. The protection was supposed to be impenetrable, and yet someone had done it.

"I don't know how. They can't take it off the grounds, though." Xander ran his fingertips over the empty space on the oak shelf. "No one can break those wards. It's tied into the grounds and the kemana."

Mara nodded and squeezed her eyes closed. The artifact wasn't too dangerous on its own. That made it even odder that they had gone to such lengths to steal it.

"Why would someone take the seeker box?" She looked around to catalog the rest of the collection. "It doesn't have that much value by itself. Not compared to many of the other pieces in here."

He frowned and joined her to check the other artifacts.

"I'm not sure. Perhaps they're one of the old guard who wishes to use it to find traitors within their ranks?"

Mara shook her head and felt relief when she saw a simple-looking dagger. That was one of the most dangerous objects known to the magical community. Only three people knew its whereabouts and it was essential it remained that way.

They made their way around the maze-like vault and checked every ward and artifact. It took them almost two hours before they finally met back at the door with grim expressions on their faces.

"I didn't find a trace of how they got in here, and nothing else is missing." Mara shook her head. "I simply don't understand."

"I fear we have been pulled into a game where we have no idea of the rules."

CHAPTER SEVEN

Xander poured himself another strong cup of coffee and slipped the potion Tori had passed him into it. He and Mara had been up with Lucy until almost sunrise, adding to the wards around the main school building and grounds. Xander had crashed on Mara's couch and managed a fitful couple of hours sleep before he was woken for breakfast. He was exhausted and didn't relish the idea of a full day of classes.

Raine frowned at the grounds which glistened under the autumn sunshine. The light gave everything a golden cast, but that didn't hide the fact something had changed. She wasn't entirely sure what, but she could feel it.

"They've added to the wards overnight." Adrien joined her at the top of the stairs to look out the large window. "Something must have happened."

"I told the headmistress about the black dog I saw last

night." Raine squinted at the horizon. For a moment, she swore she saw a shift in the defenses. "Maybe it was more serious than I thought."

"Black dogs are often tied to death, although there are a number of artifacts that utilize them." Adrien turned away. "But I don't want to be late for breakfast. Coming?"

Cameron rushed down the stairs with his hair sticking up at every angle and a crooked grin on his face. He wrapped his arms around Raine and kissed her cheek gently.

"Morning beautiful."

She laughed. "You overslept again."

He stretched before he put his arm around her waist.

"It's not my fault." He looked at Adrien. "The elf there tried to convince me that Spielberg was a better director than Kripke."

"And as I explained to the wolf, they can't be compared as Kripke is more of a tv director although he has done some movies." Adrien grinned at Cameron.

They continued down the stairs where they met up with the others.

"He did *Pinky and the Brain!*" Cameron looked aghast but couldn't hold back the grin. "That totally counts."

Everyone laughed.

"Come on, you cannot compare that to *Supernatural* or Kripke's other works." Philip shook his head. "They're completely different."

The shifter sighed dramatically. "Do you see what I put up with?" He squeezed Raine a little tighter. "It's awful. Just the worst."

She laughed.

"I slept beautifully." Sara opened the door into the dining hall. "We had the good sense to settle down for sleep as soon as lights went out."

"We might be exhausted, but we expanded our minds." Cameron ran his fingers through his hair in an effort to tidy it. "That's how I'll explain it if I fall asleep in class, anyway."

"If you ask the pixies nicely, they might give you a small coffee." Evie slipped into her usual seat. "We're fifteen now."

Cameron looked in the direction of the kitchens and tried to weigh up what his chances were of succeeding in that endeavor.

"Pancakes!" Sara picked up her fork. "I swear they know exactly what I'm craving."

Evie passed Sara the maple syrup. She proceeded to drown her pancakes in it, much to Adrien's horror.

"Would you like a spoon for those?" He pulled his crepes a little closer for fear that she might attack them with the syrup too. "I'm pretty sure you made maple syrup soup."

Sara rolled her eyes. "This is the perfect pancake to syrup ratio." She forked a large piece of them. "See. The pancakes are soaked through with rich glorious syrup."

Evie ate her fresh fruit salad and her small bowl of cornflakes slowly.

"The wards around the grounds feel weird this morning." Evie bit into a strawberry. "I can't quite put my finger on it."

"They strengthened them last night." Adrien finished his crepes. "I think it must be related to Raine's black dog."

"That black dog you saw last night?" Sara took a big gulp of orange juice. "I thought it was merely some stray."

"I'm sure everyone's parents are twitchy and they're being really sure." Philip shrugged and gave the approaching pixie his most charming smile. "You have to admit, some weird things have happened at this school."

"Hey! Breakfast was amazing." Cameron leaned forward a little. "Is there any chance I could get some coffee? I was up for half of the night engaged in a serious academic debate, and I'm exhausted."

The pixie put her fingers to her lips and thought hard for a moment before she gave a small nod and a small cup of coffee appeared in front of each of them.

"Don't make a habit of it." She took the plates away. "And don't be late to class."

Cameron picked up his coffee and breathed deeply. He drank coffee regularly at home but the school wasn't as happy about its students having caffeine.

"Ah, sweet caffeine." He took a sip. "I've missed you."

"Should I be jealous?" Raine poked him in the ribs. "Or maybe give you a room?"

He put his cup down and gave her his full attention. "I only have eyes for you."

"We really shouldn't be late for class." Sara stood. "Portals first."

Cameron drank his coffee quickly and kissed Raine softly on the cheek. "Have fun. See you in military history."

Raine ducked into the library later that afternoon after

classes to see the head librarian. She was dying to know what was going on with the school wards.

Librarian Decker looked up from his reading and smiled at her.

"Let me guess. You heard all those whispers about the wards and you came to get the gossip." He put his book down. "Am I right?"

Cameron joined Raine and put his arm around her waist.

"Are you asking about the black dog and the wards?" Cameron looked at the gnome. "Good afternoon, Librarian Decker."

The librarian ushered them to a quiet corner. He had a soft spot for Raine, but he didn't want the entire student body to hear what he was about to say.

"I'm not sure as I haven't spoken to the headmistress yet, but I'm reasonably sure something was taken last night." He looked around. "From the vault."

"There's a vault?" Cameron hissed.

The head librarian's poppy hissed and growled.

"Yes. It is a place to keep some very dangerous artifacts safe." The gnome sighed. "No one felt any ripples or faults in the wards. Don't tell anyone else about this."

"Of course." Raine nodded. "So how did they get in if the wards were untouched?"

"I'm not sure." Librarian Decker grinned at Raine. "I am, however, sure that you'll look into it this evening."

"You know me so well." She laughed. "If you have any books you'd recommend, I'd love to see them."

"They'll be waiting for you when you get here."

CHAPTER EIGHT

Raine had been very pleased to see a veritable mountain of books waiting for her when she returned to the library after classes. It took her two trips to take them to her table. She dove in and began reading from the top.

It didn't take her long to find something interesting. Cameron joined her and read with her. He was soon pulled into the fascinating history of the school and all the theories surrounding it.

"Wait, it says here some people think the Key of Solomon is hidden here." Cameron pointed to a passage. "Is that expanded on somewhere?"

Raine skimmed the spines of the rest of the books and found one devoted to that topic. She handed it to him.

They read in peace for a short while before the shifter couldn't hold back his excitement any longer.

"Have you read about this?" He gestured to the images on the page. "The Ring and Key of Solomon?"

Raine glanced at the book.

"Not yet. Are they cool?" She put a bookmark in to hold her place in the book she was reading. "They look very ancient, like three thousand years ago ancient."

"They're really cool! So, there is a heap of theories surrounding how they came about and what they really do. The humans put it down to God and other Christian theories. The magicals, however, have completely different ideas. The humans think the ring either allowed King Solomon to speak to animals or control djinn—that's genies. Now, djinn are often tied to Ifrit. The magical theory is that the ring was actually made to control the Ifrit!" Cameron flipped through some pages in the book. "There are rumors of an attempted Ifrit uprising way back in 900 BC. The ring was made to squash that before the extent of the magical presence could be revealed."

Raine read through the paragraphs around the diagrams and was pulled into Cameron's excitement.

"The seal looks really cool too." Raine pointed. "The humans think that was what he used to bind seventy spirits in a copper box. The magicals, however, think it was something else—a very powerful form of magic that was bound. The theory goes that if the box is opened it'll be like Pandora's box and that magic will be released back into the world."

Cameron shook his head. "Just once, I wish people would destroy the really dangerous artifacts rather than putting them somewhere safe."

"I agree. Somewhere safe invariably ends up being found and broken into. These people need to watch more movies and read more books."

They both laughed.

"What have you found?" Evie plopped down in the seat opposite them. "It has nothing to do with homework, does it?"

Raine pushed the book toward her friend so she could see. She felt a twinge of conscience when she recalled her promise not to tell anyone, but surely Librarian Decker hadn't included her friends in that. Their group did everything together, and she relied on their help.

Evie's face lit up. "Wow, that's really cool. And this could be hidden in the school somewhere?" She looked at them. "You know what this means right?"

"We'll look for secret tunnels and other awesome stuff?" Cameron grinned. "Because I am completely down for that."

"Are you plotting without me?" Adrien crossed his arms and looked down at them. "You know I'm the best plotter."

Evie pointed enthusiastically at the book. Soon, the entire group was crowded around the books, reading up on the theories and secrets hidden within the school they had come to call home.

The students were entirely enthralled with all the artifacts and magical objects that people thought were hidden at the school.

"These tide jewels sound really interesting." Evie handed Raine and Cameron the book. "There's a muddied view of exactly what they are and how they came about. One theory ties them into Japanese dragons, but I'm not entirely sure how. The part they do all agree on is that they can be used to control the tides. You can make tsunami and things."

"Wow, they sound really dangerous." Raine read through the text. "Imagine the damage they could cause in the wrong hands."

"They sound like they should be in the 'destroyed on principle' category." Philip didn't look up from his own reading. "There are so many of those."

"People can't help themselves." Adrien pulled down the next book from the heap in the middle of the table. "They love to experiment and push the boundaries."

"Speaking sort of that, there's a thing called the crown of thorns. Why someone would want to put that on their head, I don't know, I mean, ouch." William showed Evie the book and description. "It looks as though it gives the wearer necromancy type magic, but it always sucks on their own life essence, so they become a lich."

"Lich's are the necromancer zombies, right?" Sara looked up. "They're still undead and super creepy, but they were necromancers when they were alive and keep that magic when they turn into zombies. Is that the one?"

"That's the one." Philip cringed. "I don't get the fascination with necromancy."

"I get the one where you can talk to the dead and gain information." Raine shrugged. "The one where they raise zombies and try to take over the world is a hard no from me."

"I guess some people merely want power that badly." Adrien chewed on his bottom lip. "Back on the topic of cool, awesome things, some people think an actual flying carpet is hidden somewhere on the grounds."

"No way!" Sara leaned over to look. "I swore our professors said flying was a no go on Earth."

"They did." Raine flipped through her book. "That one has to be one of those rumors and wishful thoughts."

Sara huffed. "Shame. It'd be really cool to have a flying carpet." She thought for a moment. "It couldn't be too sentient, though. I want to control where it goes and not simply sit there and hope it doesn't dump me in the ocean or something."

"Great, now I have the image of taming baby flying carpets in my head!" Evie laughed. "I bet baby flying carpets would be really adorable."

"That raises so many really awkward questions." William raised an eyebrow. "Do you breed them? Does someone make them? So many questions..."

Sara looked horrified. "Wow, I never thought of that and I think you just killed my little dream." She shook her head. "Has anyone found anything genuinely awesome and not at all creepy?"

Everyone laughed. They were committed to the plan of finding at least the hidden passageways around the school. There was too much potential for awesome adventures to ignore.

CHAPTER NINE

Raine sat on one of the benches in front of the school building with Cameron. She leaned against him and watched the stars bloom across the clear sky. They sat in a comfortable silence.

"It feels weird when shifters have pet dogs." Cameron continued to stare across the grounds. "I mean we're not dogs, but wolves are kind of close. You know?"

Raine looked at him with amusement dancing in her eyes. "You come out with the most random things sometimes."

"The thoughts just rattle around my head."

She laughed and ran her fingers through his hair. "It does sound like it'd be weird for a shifter to have a pet dog." She looked into his eyes. "I can see it being cool, though. You could run together."

He kissed the tip of her nose.

"Maybe it's good for quieter, lonely shifters." Cameron leaned back. "Although it's rare to find a shifter outside of a pack."

A shout came from the direction of the barns. Raine and Cameron jumped up and looked around to see what had caused it. Someone ran toward them.

"He's bleeding!" Cameron rushed toward the student. "We need to find out what happened."

Raine took off after him and drew her wand. It was rare for students to get hurt at the school, and it was usually silly pranks or magical experiments gone wrong. Cameron reached the junior first and examined him quickly.

"What happened?" Raine looked around. "Are you okay?"

The boy gasped for breath. Blood seeped through his t-shirt at the side. Cameron lifted the shirt gently to reveal a shallow bite that had already all but stopped bleeding.

"This great, big black dog came out of nowhere! I was coming back from a walk around the grounds when it appeared. The next thing I knew, it tried to sink its teeth into me."

"Get him inside. I'll look for this black dog." Raine raised her wand. "He should see the nurse."

"I will not leave you out here to be attacked too." Cameron folded his arms. "If you look for it, I'll go with you."

They stared at one another for a moment with the junior looking increasingly uncomfortable.

"He needs to go to the nurse." Raine gave the student a gentle smile. "We'll escort him there."

Cameron smiled and felt victorious. He didn't want Raine to hunt black dogs which were potentially death omens alone. He had developed strong feelings for her and had no intention to lose her.

They accompanied the junior who seemed to calm as they walked. He poked and prodded at the wound while he considered how he could make his story sound far better when he told it to his friends. By the time they'd reached the nurse's office, he felt pretty good about himself and the fact that he'd fought off an entire pack of huge black beasts. That was the story he was going to tell everyone anyway.

"What happened here?" The nurse examined the junior. "This looks like a dog bite."

"Yeah. It was." The student flinched as she prodded the wound. "A big black dog. It came out of nowhere."

The headmistress arrived with her shirt rumpled and her hair pulled into a messy bun. She glanced at Raine and pursed her lips.

"Did either of you see this dog?" She gestured to Raine and Cameron. "What was your involvement?"

"We were sitting on a bench outside the school stargazing." Cameron put his arm around Raine's waist. "We heard a shout and went to help."

"Do I need to tell you to stay inside for the rest of the night?" The headmistress gave Raine and Cameron a very stern look. "I trust you'll go to the social area or the library now."

"Yes. Of course." Raine smiled as sweetly as she could. "We'll go there now."

It had taken a grand total of twenty minutes for the word to spread like wildfire through the school. As the story was told again and again, it took on a life of its own. Of course, Mark, the junior who had been bitten, only added fuel to those flames. By lights out, he was a hero who had done battle with a small army of black beasts that had tried to overwhelm the school. He'd barely made it out alive but he wouldn't let anyone else get hurt.

"What really happened?" Evie scooted down under her blankets. "With Mark. You were there, right?"

"It was a small, shallow bite." Raine laughed. "From one black dog from what I understand. He ran for his life."

Sara laughed. "I wonder what everyone will say by morning." She turned her pillow over to lie on the cold side. "I'm sure it'll be something ridiculous like a demon come to stomp on the school."

Raine was amused by the evolution of the story, but she was more interested in the fact that the dog had appeared again. From what she could recall from her reading, they were usually only seen and they didn't interact with people. The fact that this one had bitten someone made it stand out. She'd have to do more reading in the morning. She hoped to have time to ask the nurse about any magical remnants left on Mark too.

They woke up to the news that the teachers would enforce a new curfew. Every student had to be inside and accounted for by ten minutes before sunset. Raine chewed her bottom lip while she waited for Sara to finish getting ready. That meant they thought the dog only came out after dark or was at least more dangerous then.

"I heard Mollie's mom wants to pull her out of the school until this black dog stuff is resolved." Sara finished braiding her hair. "She's fighting to stay here."

"She can't afford to lose a chunk of her education like that." Evie held the door open. "Homeschooling is great, but we have some of the best professors in the world."

"I understand their fear, but I do think it's a little extreme." Raine double-checked that she had her homework. "I'm sure this black dog thing is blown completely out of proportion." She couldn't forget that someone stole something from the vault. No, something was definitely going on and she would get to the bottom of it.

Dorvu took to the skies. He had seen the black dogs creep out of the woods and slink across the open pastures when the sun set. While he wasn't sure who had brought them, he knew that one had hurt a student. The dragon fully intended to hunt them down and remove them from his home.

He flew low and made steady circles over the open ground. The headmistress had made sure all the students were indoors. He was glad to know they were safe and he was free to hunt these intruders as he saw fit. The night sky slowly clouded over and the natural light dimmed to leave only the magical light from the evenly spaced lamps. Dorvu grew bored after an hour of steady circles. He much preferred it when prey popped up quickly or, even better, ran.

He landed in the middle of the pasture and took a deep breath in an effort to catch the scent of them. They were magical, he knew that much. The headmistress had made sure that normal dogs couldn't slip onto the school grounds. These were some form of abomination.

Dorvu huffed a small puff of cold air and froze the blades of grass at his large feet. Maybe a nice nap would be for the best. The dogs showed no signs of appearing. It could have been a single strange occurrence. The more he thought about it, the more a nap seemed like a wonderful idea. He'd had a hard day of snoozing in the sun and hunting pheasants. The pheasants were more fun than the rabbits as they flew and so provided a better challenge.

The dragon's eyes closed slowly as he relaxed into the cool grass and allowed himself to fall into a light sleep. He was sure the students were safe, and a little nap would make everything go far more smoothly.

A quiet yip cut through the air and Dorvu's eyes snapped open. He smelled them before he saw them. The hounds were back, and there were a few of them this time. The dragon stood with a vicious grin on his face. He stalked toward the wood where he planned to freeze them. The gaps between the trees were a little too small for him to squeeze in there.

The dogs paced back and forth along the tree line barely out of reach of the dragon's breath and claws. One of them tried to make a run for it but he clamped his jaws over its middle and bit down. He spat it out quickly as the dog tasted awful—like soot and death. The dragon looked around for something to wash his mouth out with.

Another dog thought it saw its chance and hurtled along the tree line. Dorvu saw this as a fantastic game and ran after it and blew freezing puffs of air at it. The dog dropped dead, turned into something akin to an icicle. The dragon felt this was the fun he'd waited for and turned to look back. The rest of the pack ran across the open grass.

He took to the skies, flapped his wings casually, and found it quite easy to catch up with his prey. The one at the back looked at him and whined as it tried to run faster. The leaders split into three separate directions. Dorvu swooped down and picked up the straggler in his claws. He proceeded to break the beast's back before he dropped the lifeless form on the grass below.

The next hound wasn't much more of a challenge. He dispatched it with a quick puff of freezing cold air. It dropped mid-stride onto the grass. The dragon landed on it and crushed its fragile body beneath his feet for good measure. That left two, and Dorvu wasn't entirely sure where they had vanished to.

He took to the skies once more and flew higher to get a better view of the grounds beneath him. The two remaining dogs circled around the teachers' cottages. The dragon snorted. He would not allow them to bring harm to the teachers who had shown him such kindness. He tucked his wings back and rocketed down toward the closest hound like a large missile. The dog didn't know what hit it. Dorvu's claws struck with such an impact that it died before it could register the sensation.

The dragon walked along the ground with his wings half extended and stalked the last dog. The animal was torn between its attempt to enter a cottage and the need to escape from the dragon. Dorvu didn't want to freeze it as he found that to be a boring method of execution.

The hound tried to run around the other side of the cottage but Dorvu walked casually after it. He realized afterward that Lucy would be upset to have huge dragon prints in her flowerbeds. He'd drop something pretty on her doorstep once he was done. The dog shook with fear and tried to jump through the small gap in the window of the cottage. Its head collided with the glass, which rattled. The dragon lunged forward and snapped his teeth around its head. He spat the head out and rushed to the stream to wash the awful taste out of his mouth.

Lucy Fowler stood on her doorstep in a floral night-dress with her arms folded when he returned.

"And what have you been doing Dorvu?"

The dragon lowered his head. "The hounds were trying to get in. I removed them."

Lucy frowned and looked at the patch of black grass where the body had been. She smiled at Dorvu. "Thank you. You're a good dragon."

He perked up. "I'll find you something pretty as an apology."

"No, really, Dorvu. The thought is very kind but there's no need."

The dragon ignored that. He was already set on finding her something nice and shiny.

Mara had seen Dorvu hunt the most recent pack of black dogs a couple of nights prior. They became more frequent around the grounds. That meant someone was using the artifact. The dogs would be sent to hunt down those with secrets. The school was full of teenagers and everyone on the grounds had some secret or another. When the artifact had originally been made, the dogs would only go after those who were traitors to the coven. Given that the dog had already bitten a student, Mara knew that wasn't the case here.

Xander gathered the last of the pieces needed to create a tracking spell. Leo Decker stepped out in front of him with his arms folded.

"That looks suspiciously like the ingredients needed for a complicated tracking spell." The librarian took a step closer. "You wouldn't try to find that artifact without my aid, would you?"

The professor shook his head and smiled. The gnome was a genius with tracking spells. The ones he had woven onto the library and books were true works of art.

"I wouldn't dream of it." Xander handed Leo a bundle of herbs. "I was coming to find you."

Leo Decker took the herbs and pursed his lips. He knew that Xander had planned to keep him out of this entirely. The gnome was aware that he was the head librarian rather than a professor, but he took his duties of watching over the school and students very seriously.

They walked together out onto the grass behind the kitchens. Leo hoped they had come up with a good reason to keep the pixies out of the proceedings. They were equally as protective as him and would be frustrated to have been ignored.

"Do you know which artifact was taken?" Xander looked at his companion. "I assume you've done some digging."

The gnome thought his answer through. He knew the vault existed but he hadn't been granted access.

"I have a good idea."

Xander nodded. "Mara believes the hounds will go after anyone with a secret."

"Which is everyone." Leo sighed. "Will they kill?"

"Slowly."

The librarian's resolve hardened. He would not watch more students get hurt.

"Mark was lucky. The dog's teeth barely punctured the skin, so its venom didn't get into his system. The nurse had a healing potion on hand, so he'll be fine."

"I hear he's something of a school hero now."

Xander snorted. "Yes. I heard how that little tale grew." He shook his head. "That led to many long conversations with Agent Connor and various parents."

"I trust the parents' minds have been soothed now."

Xander nodded. "For now."

Mara was waiting for them. She had already carved the runes into the ground and arranged the candles. The tracking spell was far more complicated than those they usually worked with. The artifact had multiple layers of wards around it specifically to prevent it from being tracked.

"How did they find it?" Leo placed the herbs around the circle. "I didn't feel any changes in the wards."

"We don't know." Mara lit the first candle. "But surely it couldn't have been anyone on the school grounds."

"It must be someone with a lot of talent." Xander began adding a steady flow of magic into the circle. "A master thief, perhaps."

Mara paused for a moment. She knew what Xander thought but didn't wish to speak of that in front of Leo.

"It could well have been. Or someone with a tie to the land, perhaps." Leo placed the last herb. "Does Turner have any idea who it could have been?"

Xander's jaw tightened. He hadn't thought of that.

"No." Mara straightened. "It wasn't anyone tied to this land. Turner has already confirmed that."

Leo began adding his magic into the spell and Mara whispered the words.

The enchantment flowed around them and wound slowly into the tracking spell. They didn't have a piece of the artifact they were hunting for, which made it more difficult. Mara held the image of the jet-black cube in her mind. She hadn't seen the intricate engravings on its sides for many years, but she remembered how it felt to the touch.

Xander closed his eyes and focused on refining and guiding the spell. He felt it spread throughout the school grounds. When it located the artifact, it would ping, and they'd be able to find it.

They were all exhausted when the spell had swept every inch of the grounds and the school building with no result. There wasn't even a flicker of its presence.

"We know it's on the grounds. The wards are far too strong." Mara extinguished the candles out. "It's one thing to sneak a person inside, but it's another to break through those layers of wards without anyone feeling it."

"Agreed." Xander looked around to make sure no students were watching. "It is around here somewhere. Which means that the thief is too."

Leo sighed. "I assume you won't tell the parents that."

"No." Xander offered his hand to Mara. "They don't need to know that. Thus far, the thief isn't a threat."

"They're likely a skilled thief who doesn't intend any real harm." Mara forced a stiff smile onto her face. "The dogs, after all, won't do much damage."

"Xander said they would kill."

Mara narrowed her eyes at Xander who shrugged. "Well, that's very unlikely given none of the students are traitors," she said quickly.

Leo knew she was glossing over the reality because the dogs had already bitten a student. He merely wasn't sure if it was for her sake or his.

"Let me know if I can help." The gnome tipped his hat. "I'll head to bed now."

"Thank you, Leo. Good night." Mara relaxed a little. "We appreciate your help."

Once the gnome was out of earshot, Xander turned to Mara. "What do you really think the thief intends?"

She squeezed her eyes closed. She could feel things spiraling out of her grasp. "I'm not sure. I believe the dogs will go after anyone with a secret with the full force of their ability."

Xander nodded although he hated the confirmation of his suspicions. "Surely there aren't that many places they can hide from us." Xander entwined his fingers with Mara's. "We'll find them."

"You know as well as I do that Turner made this place to hide magical creatures. He built in secret rooms, passages, and who knows what else. Most of it isn't on the blueprints either."

"You have always loved a challenge." He squeezed her hand. "Let me take you back to your cottage. You look exhausted."

Mara ran her thumb over his and smiled. They had grown closer and she found she was happier for it.

CHAPTER ELEVEN

"I think this artifact has to be on the grounds somewhere." Raine looked at her friends. "The dogs haven't been spotted off the grounds, and the wards around the school haven't been touched."

"I agree." Adrien stretched his legs out in front of him. "I've checked the wards often with my magic and there's been no tampering apart from the teachers strengthening them."

"So where do we start looking?" Philip stood, ready for an adventure. "The woods?"

"I think so." Raine stood too. "They've been spotted more frequently around there."

The group all got to their feet and began to walk toward the front door of the school. It was a dull, grey autumn day and most of the students were curled up in the common rooms drinking hot chocolate and talking about the week.

"We have two hours until curfew." William held the

door open for the others. "We can cover a good bit of ground before then."

"We stick together." Sara looped her arm around Adrien's. "I've seen far too many horror movies to risk splitting up."

Raine laughed. "I'm sure this isn't that bad." She leaned into Cameron. "It's likely someone playing a prank that's gone a little too far."

Sara raised her eyebrow and put her hands on her hips. "You do not believe that." She pursed her lips. "After everything we've already been through, there's no way you believe that."

Raine shook her head and shrugged. "Maybe it really is a prank this time." She looked out over the grounds. "Not everything will be life or death. There will be some run of the mill, simple cases too."

Sara didn't believe her for a second. She was sure this was exactly like Adrien being kidnapped or the druids going missing. They would start doing a little digging and before they knew it, they'd be pulled into a huge, complicated plot. She wasn't complaining. There was something thrilling about saving the school. She merely wouldn't fall into the trap of believing it was simple. She fully intended to work on her offensive and defensive magic to be ready for the big showdown she was convinced would come.

They made their way across the grass and paused to look at any small indents they found to check if they were pawprints. No such luck. Raine was sure they could choose whether to leave marks or not given that she only found one pawprint when she saw the dog. They entered the woods and slowed their pace to really focus on the search.

The ground was covered in fallen leaves and the canopy overhead thinned as it went through the golden hues of autumn.

"I don't see anything." Philip frowned and looked around them for any sign of something weird. "There was a rumor that Dorvu hunted some, but no one ever found any bodies."

"In the myths, the dogs are always ethereal and capable of moving between the physical and a kind of ghost form." Raine ran her fingers over the bark of a nearby tree. "I think these are like that."

Cameron sniffed the air and smiled. "I have something. A weird scent of ash and death." He moved toward a small hollow. "Here. It was here recently."

Raine and William crouched down and carefully moved some leaves as they searched for any physical sign.

"Here. There's a mark like something lay here." William gestured to a smoothed-out area. "This suggests they were physical recently."

"I have their trail." Cameron held his hand out for Raine to take. "Shall we?"

The group felt an electricity pass through them as they set off at a steady jog through the woods. They were tracking one of the hounds. Cameron led them between the trees and skirted the very edge of the area they were allowed in. He took a sudden turn and there it was. A large black dog crouched behind a mature thorn bush.

The group moved to trap it within a circle. Evie raised her wand and began to form a bubble. Adrien and William joined her to add their spells to hers to strengthen it. The dog snarled and tried to leap forward. It hit the bubble and fell back. The group closed in around it. Raine circled slowly to see if there was something odd about it.

The dog resembled a pitch-black Irish Deerhound. Adrien looked closely at it.

"There's a very weird magic wrapped around it." He pointed toward its head. "Do you see or feel it?"

"Sorry, that's an elf thing." William gave Adrien a good-natured smile. "Fill us in."

"I'm not really sure. There's a darkness there and a binding I assume links it to the artifact." The elf sighed when the dog vanished into thin air. "Well, now we know they can vanish."

Cameron looked around, tried to catch its scent, and found nothing. The group fanned out in search of any sign of pawprints with no results.

"How did it get through our shield?" Evie pursed her lips. "It was a strong shield and should have held it."

"I'm not sure." Raine frowned as she tried to recall what she'd read. "I don't think they play by the normal physical rules."

Sara looked at her. "Do you still think it's a simple run of the mill case?" She couldn't keep the excitement off her face. "Or are we onto something bigger here?"

Raine grinned. "I think we have an interesting case on our hands." She turned back toward the school. "I'll need to do more research to see what we've gotten into."

Cameron returned to her side. "I'll be right there with you." He kissed her temple. "Every step of the way."

He wouldn't risk her trying to go into something alone.

"I can't say I'm a fan of the library but I'm down for

some research." Philip tucked his hands in his pockets. "If nothing else, I want to help make sure no one else is hurt."

"I'll bake us some muffins and cookies." Evie put her arm around William's waist. "As fuel for our long night of research."

"You are the best." The half-Ifrit rested his head against Evie's. "You know that?"

"I agree." Adrien looked over his shoulder at Evie. "We really couldn't do all of this without your amazing baking."

She blushed.

"I'm not great at research, so I do what I can." She held William a little closer. "We all have our role to fill."

Raine couldn't be happier with how their little group had come together. She was a little sad they wouldn't all join her in the FBI, but they would all brighten the world in their own way.

CHAPTER TWELVE

The students descended on the library. Leo watched in delight as he saw them move methodically through the various relevant sections. They each checked out their maximum number of books before they settled down in a quiet corner of the common room. They would have stayed in the library had they been allowed to eat Evie's wonderful cookies there.

Raine organized everyone with a notepad and pen. She made sure they each had a separate mythos and area of the world to work in so no one doubled up. They already knew a bit about black dogs, but now, they were far more interested in the type of artifacts that could summon and use them.

"I have something here." William turned his book to face Evie and Raine. "Three idols."

Raine scanned the pages and saw the sketch of the idols, three black dogs made in the old Celtic style. Each had jeweled eyes—one with rubies, one with sapphires, and one with emeralds.

"These idols were thought to be tied to the old gods. They allowed the user to summon the hunting hounds to track down people who had wronged them. They also sought out non-Celtic enemies. They vanished around the era of Boudica." William smiled at the group and felt as though he had made progress. "They could be trying to find someone who has wronged them. If you believe what people say about Professor Powell, he fills that role for a lot of people."

"That's very true. Have you made notes on it?" Raine glanced at his notepad. "It definitely seems like a strong candidate."

William made thorough notes on everything he could find about the idols. There was nothing about how to defeat the hounds. They were too closely bound to the gods, which effectively made them immortal. If that was what they were dealing with, they'd need to find and destroy or control the artifact. He suspected they would need to do that no matter what the artifact turned out to be.

Raine had chosen to look into the Greek mythos to try to find a fresh new angle there. Most of what they had on black dogs was British and Celtic. She didn't want to ignore the other areas and possibilities. An hour of reading led her down a rabbit hole about the Greek goddess Hecate. She was thought to be the goddess of witches, protection, and other things. Many modern humans considered her to be a dark goddess.

She was sure she was onto something and then she found an amulet tied to Hecate and her hounds.

"I have something!" She scribbled some notes. "Hecate

was tied into hounds. She was a goddess of protection, among other things. There's an amulet that created her hounds as protection. Someone could be in trouble and they're trying to protect themselves."

"That would explain why they came here too." Adrien looked at Raine's book. "There aren't many places as safe as this school."

Sara wrinkled her nose. "That could mean that we'll have many bad guys trying to get in, though." She returned to her own book. "I hope it's something else. I'm not ready to stand and defend the school. My magic isn't strong enough yet."

"They used to sacrifice dogs to Hecate." Raine looked appalled. "I find that particularly creepy given that she often took the form of a dog."

"There were some interesting ideas back then." William frowned at his own book. "They had a very different relationship with the gods and symbology."

"It is fascinating how things have evolved and changed over the centuries." Cameron made a quick note. "I'm glad they don't do sacrifices anymore, though. I'm pretty sure shifters would be at the top of a lot of lists and I am not ready to be a sacrifice."

"It's really difficult parsing what they actually believed because the church skewed a lot of it." Raine opened another book. "And we need to know the original beliefs to understand how the artifact works and can be defeated."

"Maybe we can get into the professors' secret library." Sara looked up. "Although it's more secret in that we can't see what's in there rather than us not knowing it exists."

"I already tried." Raine shook her head. "Librarian

Decker said it's a hard no. Even he had to fight to get into there."

"Oh, I wonder what's hidden in there." Sara's face lit up. "I bet there are some really cool books. Maybe there's even some stuff on kitsune magic. No one writes much about our magic. It's all hush hush. Of course, my family won't tell me much. They feel if it doesn't come naturally, I'm broken or unworthy."

Evie hugged Sara tight. "You're getting there. If we have to get into that library to help you, we will." Evie stroked Sara's hair. "You hear me?"

"Thanks. I'd be lost without you guys." Sara brushed a tear from the corner of her eye. "You're all so amazing."

Everyone crowded in around her and hugged her tight. Sara hadn't expected the swell of emotion from talking about her kitsune magic. She'd intended the comment as a throwaway thing and then emotions rose. The friends all held her close until she felt better about everything.

"We've only got forty-five minutes before lights out. We'd best get back to work." Sara smiled. "I don't know about you, but I have a strict one-day limit on intense research."

Philip laughed. "I'm with you there." He opened the next book on his list. "I'd rather be out doing stuff."

They returned to a quiet state of study and contemplation. It was ten minutes before lights out when Adrien struck on something.

"Hey, there's a black box thing here. It was made by dark wizards in the sixties, I think. The hounds were used to hunt down traitors to the coven and dig out secrets." He handed the book to Raine. "The hounds' bite was poisonous and they'd kill those who had betrayed the coven in some way."

Raine read through it.

"This is great." She handed it back to Adrien. "I think that one and the idols are our strongest contenders. I'll look for more tomorrow. Still, I think we should look for idols and the black cube."

Cameron laughed. "I don't think they'll have left it sitting in a classroom." He grinned at her. "But you didn't mean that, did you? You were thinking about when we find these secret passageways and such."

Raine tried to look innocent and failed. "I would never try to go against the professors' wishes and look for such passages—" Her attempt at innocence broke and she looked positively devilish. "Who am I kidding? I've already tried to get hold of the blueprints."

Everyone laughed.

"Now that is an adventure I'm here for." Philip leaned back and stretched. "Secret passageways are inherently cool."

"Agreed." Cameron closed his book. "But I am ready to crash."

Raine jotted down her last couple of notes before she, too, closed her books.

"Catch you at breakfast." Cameron leaned in and kissed her tenderly. "Sweet dreams."

CHAPTER THIRTEEN

"You know what really has me stumped with this whole missing artifact thing?" Adrien looked at his friends. "How did they get through the wards?"

"Inside job?" William offered.

"That's a scary thought." Raine frowned. "I heard one of the teachers a couple of years ago went rogue, though. He tried to steal magic from the kemana crystal."

"Damn." Philip shook his head. "That takes balls."

"And stupidity." Evie stepped into the classroom. "Everyone knows you don't mess with those crystals."

They took their usual seats in Professor Hudson's class. There hadn't been any more black dog sightings for a week and the students had pushed the teachers to lift the curfew.

"Today, you will learn a spell to disorient your opponent." The professor pursed her lips and glared at a pair of witches who were gossiping. "This falls into the category of spells that aren't openly offensive but can be very useful."

Several students huffed at that. They had looked

forward to learning something really cool and explosive rather than the simple spells the professor usually taught. Raine wished she could tell them that Professor Powell had taught her and her friends exactly that in their private lessons. They had learned how to make small objects in their environment such as berries and pebbles into small grenades they could throw or use a spell to launch at their attacker. Raine was still perfecting it but William had been a natural.

"Not every spell needs to result in bodily damage to be effective. Some spells and attacks are far more subtle than that." The professor glared at those who complained quietly. "A disorientated enemy is one who cannot attack. This spell gives you time to run or form a much more aggressive spell."

Raine had her pen ready to take notes. She was interested in making sure that her arsenal covered every potential situation. There would be times when she was an agent that she couldn't afford to blow things up or do something flashy.

"This spell will form a constantly shifting kaleidoscope of colors around your opponent. This will make them dizzy, confused, and unable to balance correctly. If they suffer from epilepsy, it will induce a seizure. With that in mind, you will be punished if you try this on your fellows outside of a classroom setting."

More whispers and huffs rippled through the students. The sophomores had been dying to experiment with their magic and play pranks on their friends. The curfew made people more uptight and that led to rebellion.

"You will begin by forming the image of a rainbow in

your mind. Once that is securely in place, press that image around the attacker in a similar manner to your shields. The next part is where a lot of people go wrong. Speak the words *contritione pervalida et confractus iris*. Place emphasis on the *confractus*. As you speak the words, visualize the rainbow breaking into shards of color that move at a rapid pace."

Raine went back over her notes and made sure she had that all down. Her visualization had improved but she still wasn't entirely sure she could pull this one off. Hopefully, Librarian Decker would be willing to help her practice. He had been okay with her throwing small explosives at him after all.

"Split into pairs and practice." The professor waved her hand. "I will walk around and help those who need it."

Sara chewed on her bottom lip. She didn't feel good about her chances of doing this spell. Something about it felt as though it would be far more difficult than it sounded on paper.

"Professor, how do we defend ourselves against this?" A Light Elf raised his hand. "I don't really want to be blinded."

The professor smiled. "That's for you to figure out."

Raine flipped back through her notebook to previous spells they'd been taught. A shadow spell seemed the most logical to her. If you couldn't see the colors, they couldn't blind you. She simply needed to weave it in such a way that it blocked the colors without blocking her entire vision.

William chose a completely different line of thought. He concluded that a spell-breaking rune was what he needed.

"You go first. I'll do defense." He turned to Adrien. "I'll try a spell-breaking rune."

"Huh. I thought of a mind protection spell." The elf gathered his magic. "Ready?"

"Whenever you are." William raised his hand and began to form the rune in his mind. "Let's see how well this works."

Adrien took a moment to form his mental image and make sure he had the words correct. When he was ready, he spoke them clearly while he pushed his magic out around William. He felt the edges of William's rune and smiled. The Ifrit was really coming into his own. Adrien remembered when he was only confident with his fire.

William watched as the colors formed in front of him, but they were muted. A clear rainbow surrounded him and where he had expected vibrant colors, they were paler pastels. He took that to mean his rune was at least partially working. The colors exploded into shards that began to spin. It was distracting but not enough to stop him from calling his own magic and strengthening his ward. The colors never quite vanished but he still felt good about what he had managed.

Raine felt the cool slippery shadow magic run through her wand and tried to direct it in front of her face. It dripped out stubbornly and formed a pool around her feet. Evie fractured the bold colors into an explosion of whirling hues and Raine's grip on her magic faded entirely. She gritted her teeth and closed her eyes as she tried to grasp the shadow. It wasn't her strong point, but she was determined to make it work for her.

Evie maintained the spell while she watched her friend

struggle to lift her wand. She knew the determined expression on Raine's face. She wouldn't give up until she had achieved her goals. The shadow crept slowly upward in thin tendrils. After a while, it formed a barrier in front of Raine and she opened her eyes. Evie waited to see if she felt it had had the desired result.

To Raine's disappointment, the shadow was too thick and when she tried to thin it, the colors shone through and confused her once more. She'd have to give some more thought to how best to combat that particular spell.

Other students tried a range of spell-breaking enchantments and runes, other forms of shadow, and someone tried fire. Professor Hudson had to step in and stop them from setting their desk alight.

"Fire is not a good defense against this." She sighed. "I recommend you think more in terms of mind protection."

The Wood Elf looked down and away and felt ashamed. He had panicked when the colors exploded in front of him and fire had been the first thing to pop into his head. Had he thought rationally, he'd have used a mind protection spell.

"Sorry," he mumbled.

Overall, Professor Hudson wasn't too disappointed. Half of the students failed to make their rainbows fracture. A few had successfully formed spell-breaking and mind protection wards, which was good progress. The others, however, were left dazed and confused by the rainbows and spinning colors. She made a note to tell Professor Powell about her results, so he could do more work on those kinds of spells.

CHAPTER FOURTEEN

"Now, remember to focus on keeping the bubble tight around your head. Think of it like really tight, thick, clingfilm." Librarian Decker raised his hand. "Ready?"

Raine visualized the mental protection growing tighter around her mind. She exhaled slowly and prepared to see the awful bright colors that the gnome had surrounded her with for the last hour. He had been very patient and explained to her how to improve her mental protection after each attempt. She had finally made real improvement.

The gnome formed the color spell once more and watched Raine's expression. Cameron had sat and watched from the nearby table and the shifter stood and growled more than once when Raine had shown distress. To the head librarian's delight, Raine grinned this time. She showed no sign of unpleasant reaction to the colors.

"I think I did it." She let her wand drop to her side. "I can't see the colors at all!"

"That's fantastic." The gnome released the spell. "Well done."

Cameron came over and hugged Raine gently.

"You did amazing work. I'm proud of you." He stroked her hair. "You'll make an incredible FBI agent."

The head librarian slipped away and left the young couple to have a moment. To his surprise, they both approached him a couple of minutes later. His poppy blew a raspberry at them.

"Librarian Decker, would you be able to tell us about the wards around the school?" Raine smiled sweetly. "I mean, how on earth could someone have slipped through them to take that artifact?"

The gnome rocked back on his heels. He'd expected this conversation. It was something he'd thought about a considerable amount himself.

"Well, there are many layers around the school and the grounds. There are crystals buried deep underground at the very perimeter. Wards, spells, and runes have been carved into the stonework of the school building and into the fence around the grounds. Further wards and spells have been layered around those. We endeavored to cover every base. There are elemental protections, mind-focused spells, shadow, light, very old rituals, and modern herbal workings. There are also more alarms than you can shake a stick at. No one should be able to look at the school funny without everyone knowing about it." The head librarian put his hands in his pockets. "I really have no idea."

Raine thought it through for a moment.

"Well, could they have had someone on the inside help them?" She chewed her bottom lip awkwardly. She honestly didn't like that idea. "Maybe they did it without realizing it?"

The gnome had thought that same thing but pushed it aside. He didn't want to think about one of their own aiding in something like this.

"To do it without realizing it, the thief would have to take control of their mind. They could then sneak in, for example, in their car if they were able to wrap the person's magic around them. Even then, that's a huge risk and would take an obscene amount of magical talent." He shook his head. "Everyone is far too careful for something like that to have happened."

"Well, the wards and all are like paper wrapped around each other, right?" Cameron asked. "So, there will be teeny tiny holes in each level?"

"In theory." The head librarian sighed. "But these are skilled magic users. Any holes will have been plugged up."

"But what if the thief did like they do in the movies with the laser grids?" Cameron looked away and felt increasingly like an idiot. "What if, for merely a moment, they used the equivalent of a mirror?"

Librarian Decker mulled it over. The shifter could be onto something. If the thief moved quickly, the grounds were large enough that the magic flow wouldn't be stopped long enough to ping an alarm. He wasn't sure what would work as a mirror equivalent, but it was worth mentioning to Mara.

"The potential is there." He nodded. "You should head to dinner, though."

Leo stepped into Mara's office and was unsurprised to find Xander already there.

"Young Cameron, Raine's boyfriend, had an idea earlier," Leo said as he entered. "He suggested that perhaps the thief did something akin to putting a mirror in front of a laser like they do in the movies."

Xander's jaw tightened as he thought it through. "It would take a lot of skill, but it could be done." He dragged his fingers through his hair. "They'd have to know exactly how all the protections worked."

"Which means someone has spent a long time studying them." Mara stood up and walked around the desk. "How did we miss something like that?"

"If they used scrying, they could have found some of the outer layers." Xander rolled his jaw. "We should have added more protections against that."

Mara put her hand on his shoulder.

"There is no point in allowing what we potentially should have done to consume us." She turned to Leo. "Thank you. We'll add further layers of protections to the wards tonight."

"I'll talk to the other gnomes. We'll help." Leo turned the doorknob. "We'll find this artifact."

"Thank you, Leo. We appreciate your help." Xander smiled. "You're valued here."

Once he had left, Mara slumped into her seat.

"Why did we not think of that?" She looked at Xander, clearly distressed. "And how have we not found the cube?"

He squeezed her shoulder. "You work very hard, Mara. You cannot be expected to be everything all the time. The hounds haven't been seen in a while." Xander offered Mara his hand. "Let's go to dinner. We can work on the protections and fresh ways to find the artifact on full stomachs."

She took his hand and stood.

"I heard the pixies are making us beef wellington tonight." She exhaled and relaxed. "They really do spoil us."

***

May had worked on her stealth spells for two weeks now. She'd made it through the curfew check and now, she was ready to sneak out. There was a boy in Charlottesville whom she'd been seeing. The curfew had put a real cramp in her plans. Still, the dogs or whatever they were hadn't been seen in what felt like forever. May wasn't convinced they'd been seen at all.

She crept around to one of the side-entrances to the school with her wand in hand. When the door was within sight, she whispered the words for the first stealth spell. It slithered over her like a second skin and made her shiver. She wove the second stealth spell as she opened the door slowly. A final look over her shoulder confirmed no one could see the door opening by itself. Next came the hard part. She whispered a spell she had been saving, overheard being used by a pixie to take the trash can out past the gate without setting off any alarms. She took a deep breath and whispered the spell, even as she opened the big wrought iron gates, squeezing her eyes shut for a moment. She slid through the narrow opening and looked back up the long drive at the main building. No lights were coming on and the only sounds were tree frogs chirping in the night. All that was left to do was travel down the lane, far enough past the spell that kept humans away. There she knew she would find Ben waiting for her.

The gate had closed with a soft snick and May was sure the worst of it was over. She ran along the grass. Ben was within sight, his pale blond hair and startling golden-hazel eyes caught in the bright light. She didn't hear it coming. Suddenly, a sharp pain seared her upper thigh and she fell. She collided with the hard, cold ground. Warmth trickled down her thigh and she groaned reflexively as she clutched her leg. She looked up and saw a black dog vanish into the darkness.

Her heart thudded in her chest. She pushed herself into a sitting position and watched with increasing anger as Ben left. He didn't even call out to her to make sure that she was okay. May stood on wobbly legs and made her way back to the school. She wouldn't make any efforts to see Ben again. As she walked and the dull pain throbbed throughout her leg, she plotted out spells and potions she could use to make him pay for his traitorous actions.

The side door flew open before May could grasp the doorknob. Her heart dropped to her stomach when she realized the stealth spells had worn off. A very angry Professor Hudson glared at her. She tapped her foot before her eyes slid down to the blood stain on her thigh.

"Come. Now." The professor put her arm around May's shoulders. "You're going to the nurse."

The professor marched her to the nurse's office. She kept her head down and tried to ignore the looks the other students gave her. The whispers rippled behind her as she started up the stairs. May shook her head. She would never take a stupid risk for a boy again.

Raine heard the news that one of the juniors had been bitten by a black dog. She wasn't ashamed to run to the nurse's office with plans to find out every little detail of the injury and the type of magic found within it. Agent Connor was there and talked in hushed tones to a number of other professors. He looked at Raine with his lips pursed. She grinned at him. Any good agent would be right where she was gathering information.

Cameron was, unsurprisingly, soon at Raine's side and they waited for the nurse to be available. Agent Connor and the teachers had moved to an empty classroom to have their discussion. Raine caught the word "parents" and sighed. The parents would be really upset about this. She would have to call Uncle Jerry once she'd spoken to the nurse to reassure him that everything was fine. Gossip like that spread like wildfire and her uncle's lack of connection to the magical world wouldn't stop him from getting word.

May was more frustrated than anything as the nurse cleaned her wound and made her drink a healing potion. The bite wasn't too deep but her favorite jeans were completely ruined. Ben hadn't tried to contact her at all. She was done with him and other boys like him.

"Are you okay? What happened?" Raine resisted the urge to pull out a pen and notepad. "What made you go out after curfew?"

May rolled her eyes. "I'm fine. It was one of those dogs. The nurse said I'll be fine in a couple of days." The girl started to walk away. "I did it for some stupid, worthless guy. I'll never make that mistake again."

Cameron held Raine close. He wasn't sure what the guy did wrong, but he wouldn't make that mistake.

Raine gave the nurse a winning smile.

"Miss Campbell. I assume you're here for details on the injury." The nurse tidied up her supplies. "It was a black dog bite."

"I gathered." Raine bit her tongue. "I'm sorry. I mean May told me as much. I hoped to learn if there was any magic in the bite."

The nurse studied her cautiously. The girl had something of a reputation as a trainee FBI agent.

"There was some. Although it was very odd magic and I can't say that I can be sure what spell it was from." She finished her cleaning. "I can tell you that it was dark magic, though. There was an edge of poison to it."

Raine grinned triumphantly. That was a real lead, something she could use when she looked through her notes on the artifacts.

"Thank you!"

CHAPTER FIFTEEN

Mara curled her legs under her and accepted the cup of sweet tea from Xander. He sat down beside her, his expression serious.

"We should make a list of potential culprits. Knowing what we now know, it should be shorter." He sipped his tea. "What about Rebecca? She had the talent."

"Which Rebecca?" Mara frowned. "The quiet little blonde who tried to sacrifice Annie or the tall brunette who constantly hit on Lewis?"

"The little blonde. The brunette didn't have the skills with wards."

Mara held her tea and let it warm her hands. "What would her motive be? And she was always more of a loner anyway. This artifact is designed for those with a coven to hunt down traitors."

Xander put his tea on the coffee table, having decided he should let it cool a little. "Are we sure that's it's only use? What if we're missing something here?" He looked at Mara. "It wouldn't be the first time."

"You're thinking of Gemma." She set her tea down next to his. "That was something very different."

She remembered the incident all too well. Gemma had been a friendly, bubbly woman a couple of years younger than Xander. They had all met in teaching college and hit it off immediately. She had the sweetest temperament Mara had ever encountered and she could light up an entire room without any effort. Everyone had loved Gemma and her vibrant personality.

It had all been an act, a very carefully constructed facade that everyone had missed until it had been too late. Mara remembered the exact moment they found out the depth of Gemma's dark magic use. She replayed the memory in her mind.

The young woman's bright smile had slipped away as her glamor flickered and crumbled. An older woman with sunken cheeks and dark eyes that resembled little more than voids stared at Mara with a look of disdain. Blood dripped from her fingertips. She had killed poor Finn with her bare hands. His heart sat on the table next to Gemma.

"You couldn't leave it alone, could you?" Gemma picked up Finn's still warm heart. "I simply help guide the local population to a better future."

She squeezed his heart and blood dripped down her pale wrist. Mara took no pleasure in what she did next. There was no choice. Gemma had crossed too many lines to find any redemption. She had lifted her wand and strengthened her resolve. The curse sat on the tip of her tongue and she glanced down at Finn's lifeless form.

Gemma had screamed in agony as the curse tore through her mind and body. She was left as a husk of what she was, entirely devoid of her magic. The police had arrived shortly after and she was taken away to a secret prison for dangerous magical criminals.

Xander stroked the back of his hand gently over Mara's cheek. "I'm here," he whispered.

Mara pulled herself out of the memory and gave him a weak smile.

"Every teacher in the school has been thoroughly vetted via Bruce and magical means." Mara picked up her tea. "We can be sure that every member of staff is safe and not the thief."

"That leaves someone from our past." Xander sighed. They had tried to narrow the list down for days. "What about Emily?"

"She didn't really blame us for what happened." Mara took a sip of her tea. "She blamed Anita and Sean. Anyway, the last I heard, she's working in France under the watchful eye of the guardians."

"Russel?" Xander picked up his tea. "He fits the bill."

Xander remembered the last time he had seen Russel a decade ago. His shields had almost collapsed under the weight of elemental magic Russel had thrown at him. The older man had been livid that Xander had stopped his plans to create a small army of vampires. As far as Xander had been able to ascertain, no one had caught him.

"I think he should be at the top of the list. He always did have a knack for scrying and wards." Mara scooted a little closer to him. "Do you remember the meal in Paris?"

"The one where we sat next to the Seine and talked until the restaurant kicked us out?" Xander smiled. "The waiters gave us as long as they dared but the manager almost bodily threw us out."

Mara laughed. "That manager never did let us step foot in there again."

Xander remembered the warm balmy night and the flow of conversation between them. The wine had been cheap and the food average, but he hadn't noticed any of that at the time. All he saw and felt was Mara's beautiful eyes and the way her face lit up when she came across a topic she was particularly passionate about.

"Do you remember when we watched the sunrise from Prague castle?" Mara smiled at him. "The way the clouds drifted slowly away and left the peaches and violets to stain the city. The snow was almost two feet deep in Holesovice, and we had to hike up those long stairs. It was worth it, though, to watch the sun rise over those red roofs coated in white."

"How could I forget?" He put his arm around her shoulders. "We stood and gazed over the city for almost an hour. The guards came and searched us because they thought we intended harm to the president or something."

Mara laughed. "They looked like little toy soldiers in their little houses." She sipped her tea. "Although they didn't appreciate it when you told them as much."

Xander grinned. "It's not my fault they had no sense of humor."

"I'm quite sure that no sense of humor is on the necessary traits list for castle and palace guards," she said with amusement.

"I suspect you're right."

CHAPTER SIXTEEN

"Today, thanks to a special request from both Evie and Adrien, we're watching *Buffy the Vampire Slayer*." Philip put the DVD in the player with a flourish. "They were both horrified that William had never seen it. It's a little modern for our usual rules, but I think everyone agreed it's cheesy enough to fit in."

"I still can't believe you've never seen *Buffy*." Evie handed William the popcorn to be popped. "It's a classic."

The half-Ifrit grinned. "Now I get to see it with you, which is better. Right?" He popped Philip's popcorn and handed it to him. "I can get the full experience with you at my side."

Evie shook her head and laughed.

"Are they eating pixie dust?" Sara pointed at the tv. "I haven't had that in forever."

"I can see if I can get some for you." Philip smiled at her. "I don't think it'd be too hard."

"Will the pixies be offended by the name?" Sara looked at Evie. "Or are they even called that now?"

"I'm not sure. I think Tori and everyone would find it funny." Evie shrugged. "If you can get some, can you get me some to give to Tori too?"

"Sure." Philip put some popcorn in his mouth. "The fashion style was very different back then."

"It's interesting how much fashion evolves and changes." Adrien ate some of his popcorn. "There are ties into the current state of society and all."

"Isn't that fascinating? How society reflects itself?" Sara glanced at Adrien. "You can look at a culture's art and learn so much about them. And yes, fashion is absolutely an art."

"I completely agree." Philip nodded. "The focuses, use of color, etc. are so important and tell us a lot."

"Wait, did she say they need to get rid of the ozone layer?" Raine frowned at the tv. "I get that they're meant to be ditsy, but I really hope people didn't really think like that."

"Why are they eating a plain hotdog bun?" William pointed at the tv in confusion. "Oh...to make that stupid joke."

He shook his head. Thank goodness he hadn't dealt with people like that as he didn't get that sense of humor at all.

"Is that such a normal thing?" Sara looked at the guys. "Sleeping with a girl then never calling?"

"Don't look at me." William put his hands up. "I've never gone that far, and I'd hope I'm far more of a gentleman than that."

"I've heard a lot of guys do that." Philip shrugged. "There's a lot of screwed up attitudes in the world."

Cameron smiled sweetly at Raine. "I'd never do such a

thing." He leaned into her. "Promise."

"Too right you wouldn't." Sara grinned at him. "She'd hunt you down and make sure you couldn't sleep with anyone again!"

Cameron paled before he laughed.

"Does that creepy guy really expect to rock up at the gym and have that cheerleader head to a graveyard with him?" William gestured to the tv. "Come on! No one is dumb enough to simply follow him. He might as well have a van with 'free candy and puppies' spray-painted on the side!"

Raine laughed.

"He's the watcher. He's important to Buffy the slayer." Evie poked William in the ribs. "He's the mentor archetype."

William narrowed his eyes. "I still think he's creepy." He ate some popcorn. "I wouldn't trust him."

"How is he the watcher when he was taken down by a brand-new vampire?" William sighed at the movie. "Isn't the watcher meant to be some badass teacher guy? We'd never respect Professor Powell if he got taken down by a small fireball."

"And, while we're on the topic, how do they explain the graves that are broken out of?" Raine bit into her Twizzler. "I mean, the normal mundane humans will see that broken coffin and all in the morning."

"Grave robbers." Adrien shrugged. "A fresh body might still be of use to medical students or organ salesmen."

"Damn, that's a weird image." Sara gave an exaggerated shudder. "Some sketchy guy showing up at my door trying to sell me new kidneys or something."

"How does that old guy sneak around the school without anyone noticing?" William waved at the tv. "I know that normal schools don't have wards and stuff, but surely people would notice a creepy old guy. He's dressed like who knows what with that long coat and funny hat. He stands out like a sore thumb."

"Magic?" Evie couldn't keep a straight face for long and she laughed. "I have no idea. I think it's one of those movie hand wave things."

"Lots of people could catch a knife!" Raine huffed. "That doesn't make her a chosen one."

Cameron kissed her cheek. "Don't worry, you're my chosen one." He grinned at her, then ducked when she swatted him. "Too cheesy?"

"It was cheesier than a wheel of muntjac. Does that even come in wheels?" Philip shrugged. "Either way, the point stands."

"It's such a waste of energy to do backflips and things in a fight. That's one of those things that really bugs me about movie fights. You have a finite amount of energy. Don't waste it!" Raine finished her Twizzler. "I know, I know. Movies aren't real life. We all have our pet peeves, though."

"How is she completely okay with all of this? One minute, she was a cheerleader with no idea about anything, and now, she's a vampire hunter." William sipped his root beer. "Shouldn't she have had some sort of a crisis or at least paused and thought about it all?"

"I don't think this is that type of movie." Adrien shifted to a more comfortable position. "It's meant to be action-focused and fun, not too much thought and philosophy."

"I'll try to stop picking at it then." William ate some popcorn. "I don't mean to ruin it for the rest of you."

"You're not." Evie rested her head on his shoulder. "It's kind of cute seeing your outrage."

The half-Ifrit laughed. He thought he would have been offended had anyone else said that, but Evie was different.

"Okay, last question." He looked at Evie. "Was this meant to be cheesy when it was new? Or is it simply how movies were back in the nineties?"

The group looked at each other.

"I'm not sure." Evie frowned before she shrugged and pulled out a new Twizzler. "Never thought about it."

William bit his tongue as he watched the guy drive into a tree. He had plenty of time to swerve but he chose to cover his face instead.

"The newer vampires seem more like zombies than vampires." Adrien pulled his blanket over himself. "The weird groaning and clumsiness. I don't remember seeing that in any other movies."

"I guess it makes sense if they haven't eaten yet." Raine drank some of her root beer. "I mean, if they haven't yet, they pretty much are zombies. They're newly risen from the dead."

"Would zombies turn into weird vampires when they ate?" Cameron looked at her. "Or is that a completely different virus?"

"I think they're related but different." Raine thought it over for a moment. "I mean, you have the whole rising from the dead and hunger thing."

"What happened to his ears?" Philip finished his popcorn. "It makes no sense for the vampire virus thing to change his ears like that. Those weird dents won't help his hearing."

Evie laughed. "William's rubbing off on you." She grinned at the half-Ifrit. "You have to let go and not think too much with movies like this. That's much of their charm."

Philip tried to switch off and simply watch. He had no problems doing that with modern movies and he wasn't sure why he found it so much more difficult with the older ones.

"That wasn't a bad movie. I can see why it's a classic." William stood and gathered the rubbish. "I'm not sure I'll watch it again."

"That's fair." Evie folded the blankets. "It's a very distinct type of movie and taste."

"What're we watching next time?" Philip looked at the others. "I think we need to go back old school."

"Agreed." Raine handed him the empty root beer bottles. "Something from the fifties. Oh, maybe *The Little Pet Shop of Horrors?* When was that made?"

"Do you mean the *Little Shop of Horrors?*" Adrien looked at her. "That was the eighties.

"Oh!" Sara put her hands up. "*Invasion of the Body Snatchers.*"

"Yes!" Evie gestured enthusiastically. "Yes. That one."

"Sounds like we're set." Philip grinned. "Anyone not want to try that?"

"I'm good."

"Me too."

And so it was decided.

CHAPTER SEVENTEEN

Raine had gathered the group in the quiet corner of the library where the less studied topics hid. There, they pored over blueprints and histories of the school.

"Turner Underwood built this mansion forever ago. It says that he kept most of the cool stuff off the blueprints." William turned the page. "I dread to think how much that cost him."

"We know there are tunnels and even secret rooms. It's merely a case of finding them." Cameron studied the blueprints again. "Did anyone see any other tunnels branch off from that one at the back of Librarian Decker's office?"

"Yeah, but he'll never let us in there." Philip frowned at his book. "Wait a second. There looks like there might be one behind the big staircase."

Everyone crowded around his book.

"We're looking for the pair of dragons?" Adrien pointed at the diagram. "And we press and turn those?"

"This is so cool. It's like something out of a movie." Sara

couldn't keep the excitement off her face. "I really hope we don't bump into anything too creepy down there, though."

"Well, Mr. Underwood did keep some weird and wonderful magical creatures here at one point." Evie grinned at Sara. "There are even rumors he had a phoenix in the basement."

"I read it was a Kraken." William's brows scrunched together. "Or maybe that was the attic."

Sara's jaw dropped before she concluded her friends were merely teasing her. Krakens and phoenixes didn't really exist, did they?

They put everything back where it belonged and tried to act completely natural as they walked past the gnomes. The head librarian raised an eyebrow and watched them. Raine was sure he knew they were up to something, but it didn't matter as long as he didn't try to stop them. They headed down the hallway toward the big staircase.

"How's baking going?" Philip looked at Evie and William. "Have you made anything fun?"

"I've mastered cupcakes and I'm perfecting my cookies right now." William put his arm around Evie. "I had no idea it was so difficult to get the perfect cookies."

"Baking walks the fine line between art and science." Evie grinned. "I love the really exact recipes, the ones where the tiniest thing throws them off."

William shook his head. "I'm perfectly happy sticking to the really forgiving ones, thanks."

Evie laughed.

"What about your art, Sara?" Cameron brushed some hair from his eyes. "How's that coming on?"

"Amazingly! I was a bit worried when I had to throw my first acrylic one out. It wouldn't come together for me, but my second attempt might be the best thing I've ever done. It's a little bit more abstract than I usually do, but I only have to add one more layer tomorrow. I feel as though it really captures the feel of a storm as it crests." She grinned. "If I can get the final layer perfect, it should feel as though you're sitting right there watching it unfurl in front of you. I used some magical paints which really adds depths. I'm incredibly proud of it."

"I can't wait to see it!" Cameron reflected her grin. "I'm envious of your talents, I can't paint a stick man."

Sara blushed. "We all have talents." She nudged him gently with her elbow. "I'm sure you have plenty."

"I'm actually pretty good with my hands. I've done some carpentry with my dad." Cameron shrugged. "You don't need to worry about my ego. It's plenty healthy enough."

She laughed.

They arrived at the back of the staircase. Philip leaned against the wooden paneling and acted as lookout while the others ran their hands over the intricately carved wood. Raine had never really looked at it before, but there was a small scene carved into each panel. One depicted a fairy standing on a hill looking out over a lush forest and another had two groups of elves meeting in the middle of a meadow.

William found the dragon scene they were looking for. He pressed it tentatively and almost jumped when it clicked. He pushed harder and it moved inwards, taking the surrounding panels with it. They peered into the darkness. Cameron took Raine's hand and led the way into the secret passage.

Philip triple-checked that no one was watching before he joined his friends in the passageway. They heard people walking up the stairs over their heads and Raine ducked reflexively. Evie and Raine formed small light orbs and they looked around them. The passage headed to their left. Cameron led them through past the plain wood paneling into the narrow, bare stone passage. A chill ran through Raine as they continued to who knew where.

There was nothing but the sounds of their own footsteps as they followed the passage in a straight line. Raine thought they must be walking past the potions labs and other classrooms. The floor began to slope downward and the ceiling lowered. The temperature dropped around them and the air grew damper.

"I was expecting something a bit more badass." Philip rubbed his arms. "Like a cool vault or an old lab or something."

Raine laughed. "These passages were made so he could move and check on his animals, I think." She ran her finger along the bare stone. "I'm not sure they'll be quite as cool as in the movies."

They continued for a few more minutes before the passage opened into a perfectly round room. Dust coated everything but Raine could still see there were engravings on the walls and ceiling. Sara used a small air spell to push the dust away without blowing it in everyone's faces.

"This is a very old spell." Adrien ran his fingertips over the symbols. "It's something my father mentioned—a spell used to contain a very dangerous being or animal."

The others looked around for any signs of this being or animal. Raine found claw marks raked down one of the walls. They stretched above where she could reach. Whatever had been in there was very big.

"Why would he keep it down here in the cold and dark?" Sara looked around them. "I don't blame it for wanting to escape."

"Some animals prefer the cold and damp." Cameron shrugged. "And maybe he tried to keep everyone safe from it."

"Maybe he shouldn't have kept it at all in that case." Evie shook her head and pursed her lips. "I know, he could have had a good reason but I don't like seeing animals in cages."

A tapping started above them. Raine frowned and looked up. Something loomed over them in the darkness. She pushed her light orb higher in an attempt to illuminate the shadows. Nothing appeared. The ceiling looked to be bare grey concrete. The tapping sounded somewhere behind them. They all spun around to see what was there.

Once again, it was nothing.

"Maybe it's time to go back." Philip started toward the passageway. "We can call this one a bust."

He wasn't ashamed to admit the place had freaked him out a little bit.

Gunnar smiled as he watched and felt the fear rise in the students. He could taste the sweet tang of it on the tip of his tongue. It ran through his magic and made him stronger, and he had only begun. His hounds would make sure that fear ran freely throughout the school and gave him untold power. Infiltrating the school and stealing the artifact had been difficult, but years of careful planning had brought success. He'd chosen the perfect place to fulfill his dreams.

CHAPTER EIGHTEEN

Sara bounced on the balls of her feet. Her four pieces of art were covered by black fabric, waiting to be revealed. There were sculptures, photography, and even needlepoint represented amongst the media collections. The kitsune was incredibly proud of the work she'd produced. She'd poured her heart and soul into them and couldn't wait for everything to be revealed. Her friends were at the front of the crowd and itched to get inside and see the show.

The organizers had brought in sparkling grape juice and Evie had made hors-d'oeuvres with the pixies' help. It felt so professional in the dining room which had been transformed to look like a professional art show. Those parents who were able to had stopped by the school that evening to enjoy the presentation. Sara's parents hadn't been able to make it, but Evie's older sister and aunt were there.

Finally, the ribbon was cut, and the crowd was allowed inside. Each artist took their place beside their art and pulled the covers off with a flourish. Sara watched her friends' faces as they looked on with awe. She felt tears prick the corners of her eyes. Evie rushed over and hugged her tightly.

"They're absolutely stunning." She squeezed Sara tighter. "I can't express how proud of you I am."

"Oh, my word, they're truly beautiful." Evie's aunt beamed at Sara. "Can I buy the oil painting? It would look magnificent in my living room."

Sara was lost for words. The organizer had said they could sell their art, but she couldn't remember the protocol.

"Yeah. I think so." Sara looked around for Isabelle and waved her over. "Isabelle, hi, erm, this lady would like to buy one of my paintings."

"That won't be a problem. How much you pay is up to you. All proceeds will go to one of three charities. Which charity is entirely your choice." Isabelle smiled. "Which painting will you buy?"

"This glorious oil painting." Evie's aunt pointed. "It's too beautiful to leave here."

"If you'll follow me, we'll fill in the paperwork." She handed Sara a sold ribbon. "Can you hang this on the hook by the painting?"

Sara hung the ribbon and felt as though she might burst. The show had only been open for a few minutes and someone had already bought one of her pieces.

Evie's sister Morgan looked at the center acrylic painting with a soft smile on her face. Sara watched as she drank in the details that she had agonized over. It was the painting she had fallen in love with. Every stroke had fallen exactly as she wanted. The emotion that she felt she'd captured within it was powerful.

"You're incredibly talented." Evie's sister turned to Sara. "You have a long and bright future ahead of you."

"Morgan's husband is an art dealer." Evie shrugged. "She's been around a lot of art."

There was something there that Sara couldn't quite put her finger on. Morgan didn't look to be much past eighteen, which seemed young to be married. Sometimes, you found the one, though, so Sara let it go.

"Thank you, but I'm going to become a lawyer." Sara tucked her hands in her pockets. "I appreciate the vote of confidence, though."

"Shame, the world needs more good artists." Morgan turned away. "Make the most of what you have while you have it."

"She's a real ray of sunshine." William glared at her back as she walked to the photography. "She's right about you being talented, though, Sara. Your paintings are truly incredible."

Raine congratulated Sara on her stunning work before she and Cameron wandered around the rest of the show. She was intrigued by the needlepoint art. She'd never seen the like of it, but she appreciated the detail and effort that had gone into it. She was looking at a photograph of a storm cresting the mountains behind the school when something caught her eye.

Cameron tensed. He'd seen the weird behavior of the senior near them too. The Light Elf constantly fiddled with the sleeve of her shirt and couldn't focus on one thing. She kept looking around as though waiting for someone to jump out at her. Cameron and Raine walked over to her with their most charming smiles.

"Is everything okay?" Raine moved into the girl's personal space and eased her away from the crowd. "You seem tense."

"I…er, yeah, I'm fine." The girl looked around with increasingly wide eyes. "Thanks for your concern."

"You smell of blood." Cameron looked pointedly at her arm. "What happened?"

The girl swallowed hard. "I can't talk about it here." She tried to walk around them. "I'll get in trouble."

"Then we'll go and talk out in the hall." Raine blocked her exit. "I'm sure we'll be able to help."

The girl exhaled slowly and allowed herself to be corralled out into the hall.

"Don't tell the professors, okay?" The Light Elf slumped against the wall. "I tried to sneak out. There's this chocolate I really like, but I had to meet someone to get it from them. It was almost curfew and one of those dogs bit me. I didn't want anyone to know that I tried to leave the school grounds. I'm already on lockdown."

"How did you get past the wards? Didn't they alert someone?"

"The wards aren't looking for who's leaving."

"Show us." Cameron nodded toward her arm. "I want to see how bad the bite is. I assume you haven't been to the nurse."

"No. I applied a healing ointment." She peeled her sleeve back. "It'll be fine."

There were black smudges around the edge of the bite. Raine looked closely and saw a soft outline of some form of symbol. She pointed it out to Cameron as she committed it to memory.

"That doesn't look like it's okay." He raised an eyebrow at the girl. "That black isn't normal. You should see the nurse."

The girl looked down at the bite and sighed. "It doesn't hurt."

The shifter gave her a distinctly predatory warning glare. She looked away.

"Okay, fine. I'll go to the nurse." She pushed off from the wall. "Just don't tell the professors."

To Raine's dismay, she had to wait until the following morning to get into the library. She and Cameron rushed through breakfast and hurried off to the library where they met William.

"I'm going into the FBI too. I want to refine my skills." The half-Ifrit put his books down on the table. "Research is something a good agent needs to be able to do."

The head librarian brought over another couple of books and the trio began their work for the morning. The rest of the group took the time to enjoy their breakfast. Raine had bounced out of bed ready to make some real progress on this mystery. She was absolutely convinced there was more to it than a missing artifact.

Cameron was surprised to find that he really didn't mind looking through the books. Raine's excitement was contagious. He loved seeing her bursting with life and hunting down a lead. The others joined them and picked up books to begin tracking down the source of the mark Raine and Cameron had seen near the bite.

"Well, it's definitely not the idols. That says the bite from them is clean. No darkness, no mark." Philip stood to put his book back. "One down."

Adrien was sure his eyes were crossing as he turned the next page. They'd gone through books, cross-referenced their notes, and dug around for the mark for hours. His stomach growled. It was definitely time for lunch.

"I've got it!" Raine thrust her book at Evie and William. "Look. The mark there. That means it's this cube created by the dark wizards to hunt down traitors. Except that mark means the definitions have been changed. The hounds now go after anyone with a secret."

"Any secret?" Evie frowned. "Everyone has secrets. Like who they have a crush on or the fact that they didn't really do their homework, or how they absolutely adore some cheesy tv show."

"Does it really mean any secret, Raine?" Philip looked alarmed. "If it does, we're in trouble. No one at the school is safe."

"As far as I can tell." Raine shrugged, unsure what to say. "It doesn't really specify if there are levels of secret."

The head librarian approached the group, sensing there was a deeper question they needed some help with.

"Librarian Decker, would you be able to tell us exactly what this symbol relates to?" Cameron handed him the book. "We're unsure if it means absolutely any secret."

The gnome frowned at it. "It does. Anything from that one time you lied about what happened to your sister's last chocolate bar through to the spell you created to rob a bank." He handed the book back. "Is this tied to the artifact?"

The group exchanged hesitant glances. Raine decided that he would have heard, anyway, and he had been a great help in the past.

"Yes. We saw it next to the most recent bite." She checked that no one was listening. "We know which artifact went missing."

Cameron pushed the relevant book toward the librarian. The gnome sighed in relief. There were far more dangerous artifacts hidden in the vault and he was sure at least one of them produced or was tied to black dogs.

"Ah, well, that's good." He smiled. "I trust this means you'll explore more hidden passages and such soon." They all stared at him, their mouths agape as they wondered how he knew they'd done a little exploration already. He simply winked, his expression deadpan.

Philip grinned. "Would you be able to help us with that?" He put his hands in his pockets. "We completely understand if you can't."

The gnome smirked and ignored his poppy, which growled. Mara wouldn't be at all happy to hear of his part in the students' adventures, but he could make sure everything was safe enough. There was no harm in them having a little fun, and he could satisfy their curiosity without putting them at risk if he directed them to those tunnels he knew weren't dangerous.

"Go and have lunch. I might have something waiting for you when you get back."

The group packed their books up and returned them to where they'd found them. Sara led the way to the dining hall, although Adrien wasn't far behind her. He was absolutely starving.

"I really didn't think you could build up this much of an appetite from research." The elf glanced back at the others. "I'm ravenous."

"Tori and everyone made fresh bread this morning." Evie fell into step with William. "I think we'll have really good sandwiches for lunch."

"I'm not picky." Adrien put his hand to his forehead melodramatically. "I think I'd eat old leather about now."

Everyone laughed. It wasn't like the elf to play the fool, but William was glad to see him with his old spark back.

***

Leo knew that Mara would give him a stern talking to when she found out that he'd given the students a guide to the safer hidden passages and rooms around the school. He felt that it was worth it to encourage their adventurous spirit. They had shown themselves to be adept and fierce fighters the previous summer and he wanted to help them grow.

The gnome walked into his office and locked the door behind him. Not even Joe knew where he hid the secret plans of the school. He'd done some digging and found them when he first joined the faculty. Leo had wanted to make sure he knew exactly how to protect his library. The books weren't the traditional gold and riches, but they held valuable knowledge that many would argue were worth far more.

He slipped behind his desk and tugged on a tiny statue

of a little silver dragon. A trio of well-worn leather books popped forward and he opened the door they had formed into his little safe. Inside were a few protective charms, an ancient gnomish artifact, and the blueprints.

Leo studied the blueprints quickly. Some of the rooms and passages weren't entirely safe, so he tucked those prints away. Then he compared the two remaining ones. After much consideration, he opted for the smaller, less detailed one. It had fewer places for exploration, but it also made them work for it. They would have to figure out the clues for themselves rather than have them handed to them.

CHAPTER NINETEEN

"Do we really have to wait until the weekend to explore those awesome new passages on the blueprints?" Sara looked back at her friends. "We can do one little one tonight, right?"

"I have two essays to write." Evie groaned. "I'll be swamped under books until Friday."

"Same." Adrien sighed. "I swear there wasn't this much homework last year."

They walked into Professor Powell's classroom and paused. A very sharp dagger sat on each desk. Raine raised an eyebrow and the professor simply smirked. She was used to them throwing magic at each other, not trying to stab each other.

Adrien ran his fingertip down the dagger and smiled. It wasn't as well made as the ones he kept at home, but it was a fine weapon and the professor had kept it sharp. William narrowed his eyes at his. He wasn't entirely comfortable with sharp objects. He knew that he'd have to get used to those, and guns, as part of his FBI training. It would take a little time, though.

"Today, you will imbue these daggers." The professor threw a dagger idly into the air and caught it, over and over again. "You will add fire magic to them. This, if done correctly, will make them cauterize the wound. If you use too much, they will become a flaming blade which will burn your hand. Not enough, and it will merely get a little warm."

An excited thrum passed through the room. This was the kind of magic the students loved to learn about.

"You will speak the words *ignis cultro* while you carefully thread your fire magic through the very heart of the blade. If you run it along the edges, it will burn itself out before you can use it. If you put it into the hilt, you'll burn your own hand."

With that, the professor sat down behind his desk and began to grade papers. He kept an eye on the students but he gave the appearance that they were entirely on their own. Having them depend on him to offer guidance and protection wasn't good for their long-term progress.

Raine looked down at her dagger and tried to nudge at it with her magic. She wanted to get a feel for its internal workings so she could better visualize how to place her power. Her magic was stubborn but did run over the dagger and gave her a view of the simple inside of the weapon. With that in mind, she chose to try to form her magic into a tight spiral down the very center of the blade. She wasn't quite sure why a spiral, but it somehow felt right. Raine assumed she'd read something somewhere.

She rolled her shoulders and picked the dagger up

slowly. Her dad and uncle had trained her to use a variety of weapons, including guns and blades. Raine was quite comfortable holding the well-balanced knife in her hand. She pulled her magic and pointed her wand at the weapon in her other hand. The image of the fire spiraling down the heart of the blade formed clearly. Her magic remained sluggish and stubborn, but it did bloom into the fire she needed.

Speaking the words, Raine pushed the spell into the cool metal. The spiral was crooked and came out more loosely than she had wanted, but it was there in place. The metal had warmed slightly, but she wasn't sure if that was a good or bad thing. She looked at the professor who studiously ignored them.

To everyone's surprise, a lump of meat appeared on a plate in front of everyone.

"Thank you, Tori." The professor didn't look up. "Your timing was impeccable."

Raine shook her head. Now, she had a way to see if her spell had worked. She pursed her lips and sliced into the lump of meat. The blade carved through it and the meat was slightly cooked on either side. It was as she'd suspected. The spell had somewhat worked.

Someone leapt out of their chair where they had put some of the spell through the hilt of their dagger. Another somehow managed to set his lump of meat on fire. The professor waved his wand and the fire went out to leave a charred black lump. Raine smiled. At least she hadn't managed to screw up quite that badly.

A glance at the clock told her she had a little more time to get it right. Once again, she formed the visualization in her mind and pressed her magic into the spiral. This time, it flowed more comfortably. When she sliced the meat again, it was entirely cooked on either side.

She was pleased to see that she had progressed at last. Her magic remained a little stubborn, but she was getting there.

"There's a passage that goes right past our room." Sara pointed at the wall they walked alongside. "That's actually kind of creepy."

"It's not like there are eye-holes there to watch us." Evie smiled. "I'm sure it's much like the other one. All dark and bland."

"What's dark and bland? I thought dinner was amazing. Wait, that was carbonara so it wasn't at all dark." Christie frowned. "I've had the most amazing time learning these new instruments and practicing for the musical. I think I need a spell to give me more time, though. I simply haven't stopped! That's not an awful thing. It's always nice to be busy, but there's something about stopping to smell the roses. I definitely haven't had any time to do that recently."

"Hey, Christie, glad to hear you're doing well." Sara smiled at the older girl. "I heard you're the lead in the musical."

"Oh, I am and it's wonderful! The costumes this year are to die for. They put so much work in, I'm sure they need more thanks and credit. Really, the musical wouldn't be the same without the costumes or the scenery. I should thank both crews more. Maybe I can get them something nice from the kemana." With that, Christie wandered off, still talking to herself.

"I don't know how she does it all." Sara opened the door to their room. "I swear I wouldn't be able to sleep with her schedule."

CHAPTER TWENTY

They had decided to try to find a passageway that appeared to lead from near the library and out to a point somewhere on the grounds. Raine argued that since the hounds were on the grounds, it made sense to look for the artifact out there. They'd concluded it wasn't above ground, so perhaps it was below ground.

"We need to press the rings in the right order, I think." William looked at the old wooden floor. "Are we sure these are the right ones? They look like coffee rings."

"It's in the right spot." Raine nudged a ring with her toe. "Any ideas what the order is?"

"Top, right, left." Adrien gestured at them. "With the words 'open sesame.'"

"You're screwing with me." Raine looked at him with a raised eyebrow. "No way did your elf senses give you that."

Adrien grinned. "I might have added in the 'open sesame' bit for a laugh."

Raine rolled her eyes and shook her head. She raised her wand and eased some of her magic into the rings as she pressed them with the toe of her shoe. To her surprise, it worked. A hatch popped open to the right of the rings.

"That elf thing is weird sometimes, you know that?" Cameron grinned at Adrien. "It's handy, though. Don't give it up or anything."

Adrien smirked. "We all have our strengths."

He stepped down into the hatch first. Sara acted as the lookout while she watched the others descend into the darkness. There was a short ladder there. Adrien and then William formed light orbs that showed a passage lined with dark marble.

"It seems a little extravagant for a hidden passage." William gestured at the walls. "Am I missing something?"

"Marble has protective properties." Raine ran her fingers over the cool stone. "It's really good for keeping things out. Or in."

Sara hurried down onto the ladder and pulled the hatch shut quickly when a couple of older students came around the corner.

"That was close." She hopped off the last rung. "What did I miss?"

"Apparently, marble's really good for keeping things in, so there could be something down here with us." Philip added another light orb to the collection floating around them. "Best keep our wands ready."

"That isn't exactly what I said." Raine looked pointedly at Philip. "I said it was good for keeping things both in and out. Meaning there could be something outside these walls we don't want getting in."

They set off down the passageway with the orbs bouncing in front of them.

"So, who do we think stole that artifact and why?" Sara didn't like the quiet as it let her think about how much earth was above their heads. "My money's on one of Professor Powell's enemies. I've heard he has a really long list of them."

"I think it's one of Professor Fowler's enemies." Adrien shrugged. "She's so sweet and quiet, there's no way there isn't a dark and dangerous past lurking there."

Everyone laughed.

"You'll be telling me you think Professor Grant was secretly a double spy next." William laughed. "Sometimes, people really are simply that nice."

"And what if she was a double spy?" Adrien grinned back at William. "You have to admit, she has an edge to her sometimes."

"I stand by it being either one of the headmistress's or one of Professor Powell's enemies." Raine leaned into Cameron who walked at her side. "They both have really dark pasts packed full of treachery and dark magic."

"How can you be sure that isn't all gossip?" Evie entwined her fingers with William's. "I mean, they're professors. If they're so badass, why aren't they out there being bounty hunters or top-secret agents or something?"

"Because the government wanted the very best to train the students in the school." Raine shrugged. "And who better to teach us how to kick ass than those who've lived it for a few decades?"

"She has a point." Cameron looked at Evie. "The school is meant to help train us up to be defenders and such."

Evie accepted that there was a very strong kernel of

truth to the stories told about them. She hated gossip, but sometimes, there was some reality woven in there.

"Are we sure this goes anywhere?" Sara huffed. "We've walked for ages and all we've seen is marble walls."

William pulled out the blueprints. "It looks like it goes out onto the grounds, but it doesn't show where it ends up." He handed them to Sara. "See?"

"Isn't that going against the entire point of blueprints?" Sara frowned at them. "I thought they were meant to show every detail of the construction."

"We know Mr. Underwood hid a lot, though." Raine shrugged. "We shouldn't be too surprised to find the blueprints aren't necessarily complete."

Sara handed William the prints and he tucked them in his bag. They continued with only their footsteps echoing around them for noise. It ate at Sara. She hated it.

He saw the students explore another passageway. The hounds had been quiet for some time while he prepared the next stage of his plan. His magic was waning due to the lack of fear around the school. This was the opportunity he had waited for.

A slow sweeping motion with his wand allowed him to send a skittering sound through the passageway. He watched in his black mirror as the redhead jumped. The thrill of fear tingled in his fingertips and he needed more.

A long, slow scratching sound followed them down the passageway. They paused with their wands up and listened. It stopped with them, which gave the sense of a deliberate, conscious action.

"What could be out there?" Sara tried to calm herself. "It's only dirt out there, right?"

"Who knows? Mr. Underwood loved to collect weird and wonderful magical beasts." Philip shrugged, then saw the look of horror on Sara's face. "It's probably a mole or something."

Sara swallowed hard and nodded. "Yeah. Only a mole."

Their orbs began to flicker and suddenly, darkness descended around them.

"Someone drained the magic from them." Adrien formed a new orb while William formed some Ifrit fire orbs. "No one is supposed to know we're down here."

Suspicion filled the elf. They'd been careful. The gnome knew, but he had been a strong ally in the past. It didn't make any sense for him to toy with them like this.

Heavy footsteps charged toward them. They pulled their magic and formed a wall of fire in front of them. Raine stood at the front of the line with Cameron and William on either side of her. Adrien gripped his sword tighter. He hated that he was pushed from the front line.

They waited and waited. Nothing came. The noise vanished. Sara's heart rate began to slow.

"Someone knew we were here." Raine turned to her friends. "And they tried to scare us."

CHAPTER TWENTY-ONE

The group hadn't tried exploring any new rooms or passages for a week. Raine refused to let go of the idea that someone had screwed with them, but they had no idea who or why. They finally concluded it must have been a senior or another older student who had seen them head down there.

The black dogs hadn't reappeared, and the professors were beginning to crumble beneath the students' pushes to remove the curfew.

"I really think that whatever was going on has cleared up." Sara shrugged and chewed on the end of her paintbrush. "I mean, no one else has been bitten. The dog-hound things haven't been spotted in a while. It's horrible being tied to a curfew every night."

"It's too weird for them to simply vanish like that." Raine passed Sara the water glass. "I think they're waiting for something."

"You're too suspicious." Sara gave her a gentle smile.

"Not everything has to be life and death or the end of the world as we know it."

"They could have gotten the artifact off the school grounds." Cameron looked at the bouquet of flowers Sara had painted. "That would explain it too."

"Yes!" Sara pointed at Cameron with her brush. "Maybe that. They got onto the grounds without anyone noticing anything weird in the wards. So maybe they got back off too."

It didn't sit right with Raine, but she let the topic go.

"Are you about ready?" Philip walked into the art room. "The dinner starts in ten minutes."

"Seriously?" Sara dropped her paintbrush and rushed to the closest cleaning station. "I completely lost track of time."

"Evie's baked up a storm." William stepped around Philip with a proud grin on his face. "She said she's mastered choux buns. I'm not sure what they are, but they sound really good."

Sara washed up quickly. Raine helped her scrub some paint off her cheeks before they all headed to the dining hall for a new tradition. The headmistress wanted to celebrate the new school year and bring everyone together. The older students had pulled out all the stops with the decorations. Small trees stood in the corners and the fresh scent of autumn filled the air. Elegant centerpieces sat in the middle of each table. A large candle was the focal point of the one on the group's table.

Raine sat down and smiled as she watched Sara peer at the centerpiece.

"That glasswork is incredible!" She pointed at the very

fine weaving of the glass threads to form a pale golden basket. "Look at how realistic those fruits look too."

Raine had to admit it was a real work of art. The glass had a soft sheen to it that showed it was glass without taking from the realism. The colors were vibrant and eye-catching. Every line was perfect, with not a single mark of imperfection on it. The candle lit of its own accord and that was the signal for the first course.

Evie joined them with a huge grin on her face. "You'll love it!" She took a sip of her water. "Seriously, this is one of Headmistress Berens' better ideas. Nice way to bring everyone together early in the school year."

The spicy squash soup appeared in front of each student. A small pumpkin had been drizzled in fresh cream in the middle. Raine wasn't sure how they managed that. Even with magic, it was a feat in her mind. As she enjoyed her soup, she looked around and admired the leaves that fell from the ceiling. Each time they reached barely above head height, they vanished and reappeared at the ceiling again, ready to fall in slow motion once more. There was a rustle and a soft breeze which wrapped the feeling of autumn around them.

The decorations were simple, but Raine enjoyed the little touches. The scents and sounds really brought about a sense of the changing season and made her feel content.

The main course was an extravagant meal of turkey with all the trimmings. Cameron took his time to enjoy the turkey.

"Why so much turkey so early in the year?" asked Evie.

"Who cares?" Phillip's eyes widened at the sight.

"I'll trade you my mac 'n cheese for the last of your

turkey." Cameron lifted his mac 'n cheese toward Adrien. "Deal?"

Adrien looked at his plate. He wasn't a big fan of turkey, but he didn't much enjoy mac 'n cheese either.

"I'll trade." Evie lifted her turkey. "I love mac 'n cheese."

Cameron grinned victoriously, and they exchanged their servings of food. The shifter kept the cranberry jelly to one side and ate it as a small dessert rather than a relish. Philip shook his head but said nothing. He couldn't imagine eating his turkey without a large helping of cranberry jelly.

There was a peaceful lull once the main course plates had been taken away and small cards with elegant copper script appeared in front of everyone.

Today we come together as a community. A family in gratitude for all we have and all that is yet to come.

Evie smiled.

"Tori wasn't feeling all that subtle this year." She held her card up. "I'll go first. This year, I am grateful for my amazing friends. The progress I am making in my chosen skill sets, and last but not least, my incredible boyfriend William. He has brought light and joy to my life in ways I could never have expected."

William blushed before he leaned in and kissed Evie on the cheek. "I'd be lost without you." He looked into her eyes. "You've helped me see the potential I hold and how to fulfill it."

Philip cleared his throat. "We are a community and this new school year, I am grateful for this fantastic school and its dedicated professors. They listened and gave us the very best curriculum. I'm also grateful for my friends, our movies nights, and the laughter we share."

Raine held up her card. "I'm thankful for all of you. For the opportunities I've been given, and the experiences we've shared together so far. I'm thankful for the support and affection Cameron gives me, and for the chance to have a relationship with such an amazing guy. Oh, and for the gnomes. They've been instrumental in my progress with my magic."

Cameron put his arm around Raine's shoulders. "I'm thankful for you guys, my adopted pack. I'm thankful for all this school has given me. I have finally found a home away from home and can see a path toward a bright and happy future. I couldn't have done any of that without all of you. And I'm thankful for Raine. Her strength, perseverance, and passion have guided me and made my life happier."

Mara looked around the professors whom she was lucky enough to call friends. She lifted her wine glass and smiled at Xander.

"Today, we recognize how important our school family is and how much we always need to work together." They all shared a toast. "Through cooperation, we help shape the future through these talented students. Long may that continue."

Xander took her hand under the table. He and Mara grew slowly closer and he found that he sought out contact with her more and more. The little touches brought a gentle smile to his face and filled him with a happiness he hadn't felt in many years. That day, they allowed the worries and concerns of the artifact to be forgotten and focused on the joy they were surrounded by.

The pixies spoiled them all with an array of pastries, pies, and small cakes. Xander bit into a particularly rich and sumptuous chocolate pie with a look of absolute bliss on his face. This brand-new tradition was a day of celebration and he was particularly thankful for the family that surrounded him.

CHAPTER TWENTY-TWO

Adrien felt a little weird going into the Louper game knowing that the threat of the hounds was still present. He looked into the crowd and saw the happiness present there. The Louper game gave everyone a break from the pressure of classes and any tension the hounds might still bring. He smiled and felt a weight lift. This was a good thing. It was something everyone needed. They were so close to moving up in the rankings.

Etienne patted his brother on the shoulder and grinned at him. "Relax, little brother. We'll kick ass."

Matt led the team out onto the field and Adrien felt the excitement wash over him. Whatever nerves and concerns he might have had slipped away and left him ready for the match to come. They were in the final ranking which meant the match was likely to be more difficult.

If they could pull this off, they'd go into the opening ranking for the national championships in the next semester and on to the world games. He looked at his friends who all waved and cheered him on. They needed this win as much as he did.

The team stood close together and waited patiently for the game to descend. It took longer than usual and Adrien hoped the hounds wouldn't interfere with that too. He drew his sword reflexively from the ether in preparation. Thankfully, the field transformed into something else. At first, he thought it was undulating snow but then Adrien realized it was, in fact, cloud.

He looked at the crystal blue sky around them and the soft white cloud beneath his feet. Scientifically, the cloud shouldn't be able to hold their weight, but there it was. He wouldn't complain and really wasn't in the mood to fall to his doom. Ahead of them, a pure white city grew from the cloud-base. Clear, strong lines formed bold buildings with glints of glass and a brilliant sheen that almost blinded Adrien. He formed a soft shadow spell over his eyes to act as sunglasses.

Cody and Daniel looked suspiciously down at the cloud they stood on. They weren't at all convinced that it wasn't a big trap. Etienne and Matt had already headed out across the snowy white pillows toward the city, so they had no choice but to follow. They copied Adrien and formed thin shadows across their eyes to help handle the glare of the light.

The city was far closer than Adrien had initially thought. Everything was pure white, and it hurt his eyes even through the shadow. It felt cold and unwelcoming, he couldn't imagine spending very long there. Odd bird people walked along the streets. Feathers fell where hair would have been on a person. They were dressed as people, but they were very clearly birds with clear beaks and long bird legs.

The elf shook his head and looked around for any clue of where the gold token was. He looked skyward even though he realized everything was skyward when you were in a cloud city. There was no obvious sign of the gold token anywhere along the roofline or in any of the windows. He hadn't expected them to make it easy, but that didn't stop him from hoping.

Matt paused in the middle of the street and tried to make sense of what his shifter instincts told him. The token felt as though it were below them somehow. He frowned and looked around for some way to get down from or through the cloud. His instincts pushed him forward and he led the team around a tall, slender building into a narrow alleyway. There, a ladder descended through the cloud.

The elf brothers approached it with their swords drawn. It felt too good to be true. They peered down the ladder into the whiteness below. There were no signs of any traps, but that didn't mean they weren't present. Matt took the risk and started down the ladder. His instincts told him that was where they needed to go. They couldn't afford to hang around debating if it would bite them or not.

The shifter reached the bottom of the long ladder and stood on the top of a far darker cloud. Lightning shot beneath his feet with only a thin layer of grey between him and it. That made him nervous and he set off at a jog the moment Cody's feet hit the cloud.

Something gold glittered in the distance, and Matt had

some hope that they had made real progress now. He hated not being on solid ground. It felt completely wrong. Shifters were meant to run on nice dirt, not weird clouds. Adrien remained at the back of the group and watched over everyone with his sword drawn. Something felt wrong. He saw the glint of gold, but he also saw the lightning.

The cloud beneath them shifted and Adrien realized it had begun to swirl.

"Run!" he shouted.

The wizards didn't so much as glance back but raced off as fast as their legs could carry them. They'd learned to trust Adrien and the elf was glad for it. He hurried close behind them while he kept a close eye on the swirling cloud. It seemed to follow them. Its movement shifted from light undulation to bubbling upwards. Adrien had a horrible feeling they were about to be chased by a tornado.

Raine watched in horror as a small cluster of tornadoes bubbled up from the cloud behind the team. They seemed almost sentient as they moved to corral the team into the darker area of the cloud where the lightning burst upward. Matt led them valiantly across the cloud and they ducked through a gap in the tornadoes, but it wasn't over yet.

Evie gripped William's hand tightly as they watched from the edge of their seats. The tornadoes closed in, but Cody and Daniel tried bravely to fend them off with air spells of their own. One of Cody's spells broke through and a tornado disintegrated.

Matt took a sharp turn toward the gold token, but it was in the middle of the very darkest cloud where the lightning arced upwards into the clouds above them. The shifter didn't even hesitate. He felt as though he understood the pattern of the lightning and ran with everything he had, darted around a stray bolt, and dove onto the gold token. His breath came in sharp gasps, but he'd done it. The token was in his hands and no one had been caught by the lightning.

He felt ready to kiss the earth when the field materialized beneath him. He'd never been so glad to feel solid ground before. His kind were not meant to be up in the skies. It was wrong and a crime against nature. Adrien helped him to his feet as the crowd descended onto the field. They'd done it. Moving up in the rankings was in the bag.

CHAPTER TWENTY-THREE

A scream cut through the air. Raine jerked up in bed and looked around to make sure her friends were okay. Christie was still fast asleep, but Evie and Sara had also sat up. Raine reached for her wand and scrambled out of bed. Whimpering sounded from the hallway followed by rapid footsteps.

The girls moved silently. Raine opened the door and peered around it, unsure of what she expected to see. A large black hound hurtled past them. Raine watched in horror as it chased an older witch down the corridor. The girl spun and tried to throw a spell at the animal. The magic went right through it as though it wasn't there.

Raine stepped out into the hallway with her wand raised. Spells cycled through her mind as she chased after the hound, determined to save the witch. Evie and Sara were close behind her as she turned the corner. The witch had been cornered. She threw spells at the hound but nothing seemed to work. A large fireball left a charred mark on the wall.

"We contain it." Evie raised her wand. "The bubble worked in the woods."

The girls spoke as one as they pushed their combined magic into the bubble spell. It encircled the hound and held it in place as it snapped and snarled.

The witch it had chased sighed in relief. "I don't know why I didn't think to contain it." She smiled. "Thank you."

"Now what do we do with it?" Sara kept her hands raised. "I don't know any hound banishing spells."

"And the last one slipped out." Evie took a step closer. "We need something to either kill it or tether it, so the professors can help."

The hound dissipated in a small wisp of black smoke and left no sign it had ever been there. The older witch's eyes went wide. Another scream echoed in the silence. Raine burst into the room on her right. A Light Elf sat bolt upright in her bed, her eyes wide in terror.

"It came for me. I ran and ran, and I couldn't get away." She gulped down air. "I can still feel it. It won't leave me alone. I don't know what it is, but it won't leave me alone."

"You're safe." Evie went to the girl. "It was only a nightmare."

Raine had barely gotten any sleep. Screams echoed constantly from the rooms around them. Footsteps and yipping raced down the hallways. She heard Professor Hodges call out from somewhere nearby, but it didn't make her relax at all. Scratches sounded from the doors and walls. Evie passed out some vitality potions and everyone knocked them back gratefully with their breakfast.

Cameron remained close to Raine. He wanted to know that she was safe and well. Philip rubbed at his eyes and looked around blearily.

"I miss sleep." He took a bite of his pancakes. "I don't think I slept a wink."

"Me neither." Adrien sighed. "Every time I started falling asleep there was more screaming and footsteps."

"I heard the entire school was wracked with nightmares about those hounds last night." William drank his orange juice. "I think the professors are looking into increasing protections again."

"How did they even break those the existing protections?" Raine frowned. "There are so many layers of them. I don't understand."

"And why now?" William looked at her. "Whoever's controlling them must have a reason for this timing."

Raine rolled her shoulders and thought about it. The half-Ifrit was right. She needed to try to see the big picture and think this through logically. What did the artifact thief get from bringing the hounds into the school now?

"Well, they're not looking for one specific person." Evie brushed some hair out of her eyes. "Nearly everyone was struck by nightmares."

"And the hounds didn't seem to discriminate as to who they chased around the school." Adrien finished his crepe. "Which suggests they're aiming for something larger. Do they want to drive us out of the school?"

"Or deprive us of sleep? We'll be easier to control if we

can't sleep." Sara pushed her empty plate away. "They could have some grand puppet-master plan."

"Why now, though?" Raine leaned against Cameron. "What was special about last night?"

"Maybe they needed to gather some stuff before they could do this." Philip dragged his fingers through his hair. "Some of those rituals are crazy complicated and need all sorts of weird ingredients."

"If he's doing a ritual, he'll need a reasonably large space." Raine chewed on her bottom lip. "We might find something on the blueprints."

"Don't ritual spaces need to be cleansed and have certain things?" Cameron looked around the group. "To, you know, hold the magic and stop it getting corrupted and stuff."

"You're right, we learned that last year." Raine tried to think if she'd read any relevant rituals during their research. "I'm not sure what spell would work here."

"We're looking for a hidden room? Somewhere quiet, magically clean, anything else?" William looked at his friends. "Does it need a window?"

"We'll have to do some research." Raine stood. "Sorry. I don't know much about ritual working spaces."

Cameron slipped his arm around her waist. "You don't have to know everything all the time." He kissed her temple. "You're still human."

William reached over and squeezed Raine's arm. "I'm sorry." He gave her a small smile. "I hadn't meant that you should know everything. But you've done so much reading on this artifact."

She nodded. "It's okay." She started toward the library. "I'll see what I can dig up this morning."

The others joined Raine, William, and Cameron.

"I need a good, strong wake-up potion. My eyes will cross when I try to read," Philip groaned. "I don't remember the last time I was this tired."

Once they were somewhere quieter, Evie pulled a small vial of dark blue liquid out of her pocket.

"I've been practicing brewing them." She handed it to Philip. "I thought they were useful to know."

"You're a savior." Philip drained the liquid quickly. "We'd be lost without you and your potions genius."

Evie blushed before she handed the others a vial. "Don't worry. These are okayed by the headmistress." She drank her own. "She knows I make them and is fine with me giving them to you guys. No more than two a day, though."

"We'll need them if those hounds keep up this pace." Cameron sniffed at his vial before he drank it. "Do these normally taste so good?"

"No." Evie grinned. "I added in a little something extra. They usually taste like dirt."

"You're far too good to us." William squeezed her a little closer. "We really don't deserve you."

Raine felt the effects of the potion a few minutes later and was pleased that her head had cleared. She started to run through what she knew so she could focus their efforts on the right areas of the library.

"We'll need to split up and look at the blueprints and ritual workings." Raine opened the door to the library. "I'll see if Librarian Decker can help us too."

The head librarian saw the students come in and smiled to himself. Raine had the look of determination on her face that he had come to associate with her sinking her teeth into trouble.

"And what can I do for you today?" His poppy blew raspberries. "You seem to be on a mission."

Raine smiled. "We have concluded that the artifact must be within the school. Given that the hounds are now terrorizing the students, we feel it's imperative we find and remove the artifact." Raine held his gaze. "Would you be willing to help us with that, Librarian Decker?"

He had told her to call him Leo, but she never dared to around her friends. He didn't mind as he didn't know them as well as he knew her and liked to keep some air of professional distance.

"On the condition that I join you on this little adventure." He tried to hide his broad smile. "I have some blueprints that might help you."

Cameron bit his tongue. He'd suspected that the blueprints they'd been given didn't show quite everything. The gnome had his reasons to hide them, though, he was sure.

They followed him into his office. Raine remembered the last time they stepped foot in there. They had performed the tracking spell to find Adrien. She glanced at the elf who looked at the bookshelves with quiet awe. Raine was glad to have him there with them that time.

The gnome pulled another set of blueprints out of a hidey hole that Raine didn't quite manage to see. She smiled. He had clearly used a glamor to hide his secrets.

She intended to ask him about those so she could use them herself. Being able to hide important things was a useful skill. Even if those important things were merely her chocolate stash.

He laid the blueprints out on his desk and the students gathered around.

"Any ideas what exactly we're looking for?" He looked at Raine. "I assume you've done some research."

"We're looking for a ritual space, we think." Raine studied the prints that showed far more passages and rooms than the ones they had. "The thief is using the artifact, after all, which means he needs a space to do that in."

The head librarian nodded.

"There are so many hidden rooms on every level." Cameron frowned as he examined the prints to see if something stood out. "How do we know if they might be suitable for rituals?"

"The room will need to be balanced. It can't be an odd shape or have windows on only one side." The gnome pursed his lips and looked at the basement level. "It doesn't need a window, and it really depends on the magic worker. Each species has their own preferences to make it more complicated. Gnomes prefer to be underground but elves prefer higher rooms. Wood Elves want to be able to see nature and Light Elves like to see the sky."

"We have lots of options." Raine tried to be logical about it all. "Why don't we start from the passage closest to the girls' dorms and go from there?"

They had seen at least two hounds around the girls' dorms, so it seemed like a solid place to start.

"There are a number of rooms we can reach from this

passage." The head librarian pointed at the one closest to Raine and her friends' room. "Two of them fit the criteria for ritual rooms. The problem is, most of Turner's work required ritual work and runes to deal with the animals he kept."

"Meaning we have a number of options to look through." William put his hands in his pockets. "I assume there are no spells we could try?"

The gnome shook his head. He and the professors had already exhausted their arsenal of tracking spells.

"I'm afraid not. It's down to time and patience. We need to check every viable room." He rolled the blueprints back up. "Shall we?"

Joe waited for them outside the office door. He stood with his arms folded. "Were you going adventuring without me?"

Raine covered her smile with her hand as she didn't want to upset the gnome.

"Of course not." The head librarian grinned. "I was about to call you."

Joe narrowed his eyes before he accepted it and stepped aside. "Where are we off to then?" He looked at the gathered group. "I assume we're tracking down this artifact."

"We'll start in the passage near the girls' dorms, then head to the hexagonal room." Leo headed off through the library. "We need rooms suitable for a ritual."

"There are plenty of them." Joe nodded. "Are we expecting trouble?"

"No." Leo shook his head. "I'm sure it'll be nice and easy."

Cameron wasn't so sure that it'd be nice and easy. His

shifter instincts told him they had missed something, or perhaps even worse, were walking into a trap. He put his arm around Raine's waist and said nothing. He didn't see a reason to worry the group when it might prove to be nothing.

Mara pressed the small carved flower and smiled as the stone around it creaked and groaned. She hadn't wandered the hidden passages and rooms of the mansion in a while. There was something thrilling about it. After the hounds had begun to prowl the school itself, she and Xander had decided it was time to be more proactive about finding the artifact.

He helped move the stone door aside and followed her into the darkness. Mara cast the light spells while he pulled the door closed with a heavy snick. Torches along the stone walls all lit up in response to her magic. They would never burn down, not while someone magical walked that particular passageway.

The damp air clung to the pair as they walked along the narrow passage. Xander kept his wand raised, ready for hounds or worse that might try to attack them. Given the number of secrets he carried, he knew the poison would hit him hard and fast. He had been poisoned before and had no intention to repeat the experience. Something felt very wrong a few minutes into the walk when a sharp left turn came into view up ahead.

Shadow dripped from the ceiling and slowly consumed the light from the torches hung evenly along the walls.

Mara slowed her breathing and tried to feel for any strange magic in the area. Turner Underwood had kept most of what he did within those secret spaces hidden.

Xander resisted the urge to immediately banish the shadow and allowed it to continue to ooze from the ceiling as they approached the corner. He wanted to see exactly what it planned and get a better feel for the magic that ran through it. If he could find a unique magical signature, it might help tell him who the thief was.

They went to turn the corner and found a wall of pitch darkness. Mara shook her head. She had faced far more terrifying things when she had been stuck in the World in Between. She stepped into the darkness with her magic thrumming through her, ready to be used should she need it. Xander followed her with his teeth gritted. Her fearlessness concerned him at times and he wanted to keep her safe. He knew far better than to try to act like her knight in shining armor, though. Mara was a very capable magic user and a strong fighter.

He was barely four steps into the shadow when he felt thin threads of magic running through it. Immediately, he latched onto them and tried to trace them back to their source. The shadow suddenly lifted in barely the blink of an eye. Xander sighed.

"I think we're being tested." He looked at the ceiling. "I felt threads of magic but I wasn't quick enough to track them."

"Now we know that whoever the thief is, they are tracking us and our whereabouts." Mara looked back at him. "Which tells us they're skilled in tracking."

"That knocks Rose off the list. She was a good seer but

couldn't form a tracking spell to save her life." Xander ran through his mental list. "The others were all good at tracking, though."

"We're one step closer." Mara continued down the passageway. "Every step helps."

Raine followed the head librarian into the first room. It looked like any other area around the school if you ignored the complete lack of furniture. She wasn't sure how people had missed the fact that they couldn't access it. There were two sets of windows where the walls formed a corner. The floors were bare wood, and the walls were remarkably clean. Pale cream wallpaper shimmered with light golden patterns Raine couldn't quite make out.

Small scuff marks on the floor suggested that furniture had been there once and moved around. Now, it stood entirely bare. Cameron looked around the room and sneezed as the thin layer of dust affected him. The windows looked out over the back of the grounds. He thought they were over the kitchens, but he couldn't hear a single sound outside the room. Absolute silence reigned.

"Why would they soundproof this room?" Cameron looked at Librarian Decker. "I can't hear anything outside of this room."

The gnome looked around and pursed his lips. His mind flitted to dark theories full of blood and heartache.

"Perhaps there was an animal with a dangerous cry in here." He gave a weak smile. "Something that would harm others should it have been heard."

Cameron walked around the room with his ears pricked. He saw Raine inspect the wallpaper, but his instincts told him there was something in that room with them. The shifter couldn't quite be sure what it was or where it was, but his hackles stood on end. Something skittered across the ceiling above his head and he bared his teeth reflexively, ready to attack.

Everyone paused and looked up.

Suddenly, a swarm of scorpions flooded the room from a pinpoint in the middle of the ceiling. They scurried across the white paint and dropped down around the students. Raine didn't intend to waste time waiting to see what they would do. She pulled the fire spell into her mind and William stepped beside her. They set the scorpions alight as they tried to run across the floor toward the students.

Cameron stomped on those they hadn't reached. Sara jumped back when one began to climb up her leg. She threw an air spell at it and launched it into the far wall. The students and gnomes scorched the entire room to leave blackened husks in their wake. Raine felt herself and her magic grow tired and the scorpions still spilled into the room.

She wouldn't give in that easily and joined Cameron in his crusade against the scorpions, stamped on them with everything she had, and hoped her energy would return to her soon. The others grew equally as tired. Evie froze when a scorpion landed directly on her head. She looked at William with wide-eyed terror. He reacted without thought and directed a thin stream of Ifrit fire directly at it.

The scorpion's charred remains dropped off her head and he ran to hug her tightly.

The students had no choice but to stamp on the creatures as exhaustion overcame all of them. Fear began to rise within them. They grew increasingly tired, and they were stuck in that room with thousands of scorpions.

Raine looked at the door into the room and debated whether they would be better off if they tried to run. Then, as suddenly as it had begun, the torrent of insects stopped. Their bodies, which had covered the floor, vanished and left everything exactly as it had been when they walked in.

"Someone was playing with us." Raine was livid. "They know we're trying to find them."

CHAPTER TWENTY-FOUR

They retreated down the passageway when Raine bent and picked up a dark almost black-colored ring with an odd crest on it. She put it in her pocket to take to the headmistress as she thought it might be something Mr. Underwood might have dropped at some point. The exploration had been fruitless and she was irritated that the thief felt they could play with her and her friends. Still, there wasn't much to be done about it.

The head librarian led the group into the main school. He didn't want them gone too long. Mara would already give him another talk if she found out he'd led them into the passageways to begin with.

"Enjoy lunch." He smiled at the group. "We'll try again soon."

Raine itched to go back into the passages directly after lunch. They still had the other set of blueprints and there were plenty of places on there they hadn't explored yet. She smiled at him.

"Thanks for your help, Librarian Decker." She looked at

her friends and back at the gnome. "We really appreciate your help."

The others echoed the sentiment before they headed down to the dining hall. Raine plotted which passageway to try next as they walked. She wouldn't give up on this case yet.

Raine and Cameron went to the headmistress's office after lunch. She held the ring in her hand and felt she was doing the right thing. It looked valuable and likely magical, and Mr. Underwood must have missed it. Cameron knocked on the office door and they waited.

"Should we tell them where we found it?" He looked to Raine. "We'll probably be in trouble."

Raine hadn't decided quite what to do. On one hand, telling them would get them in trouble. On the other, if they found out she'd lied, they'd be in even more trouble.

The headmistress opened the door. She wasn't surprised to see them. "Did something happen?" Ms. Berens looked expectantly at them. "More hounds?"

Raine seemed to have a way to find trouble and her tenacity meant she was quickly at the very heart of it.

"We found a ring and we think it's Mr. Underwood's." Raine held her hand out. "It looks like something he'd miss."

The headmistress paled and took the ring. She showed it to Professor Powell whose face darkened.

"Where did you find it?" The headmistress ushered them into her office. "Raine, where did you find this ring?"

Raine and Cameron looked at each other.

"In a secret passageway." Raine straightened defensively. "We were looking for the missing artifact."

The headmistress sighed and shook her head. "Students are not allowed in there. You are grounded. You will not go anywhere but your classes, the dining hall, the library, and your dorm room." She picked up her phone and dialed Agent Connor's number. "This is more serious than you realize."

Raine gritted her teeth. She felt that the headmistress had overreacted and she certainly wouldn't stop her search for the artifact.

"We understand that you plan to become an FBI agent." Professor Powell approached them. "But this is something the professors need to deal with. It is not a matter for students."

She said nothing. Students were being haunted and harmed and she couldn't sit by and wait for the professors to resolve the problem.

"Agent Connor will be here momentarily to speak to you." The headmistress leveled a glare at Raine. "How did you find out about the passages?"

"I read about the history of the school in the library." Raine shrugged. "Some of the books mentioned them and I managed to follow the clues."

She wouldn't get Librarian Decker into trouble. He had been a kind and generous mentor.

Agent Connor walked into the office and looked at Raine with disappointment etched on his face.

"Raine, what would your uncle say about this?" He folded his arms. "You should have known better."

"My uncle would be proud of the fact I tried to help my fellow students." Raine folded her arms in a mirror of his. "He would be happy to see me take the initiative."

"I'm sorry." Agent Connor sighed. "I am supposed to guide you on your path to become an FBI agent, but I have failed you. A good agent doesn't go off half-cocked and try to do things behind their superior's backs. They keep their team up to date and ensure that everyone is safe."

Raine looked away and barely listened to the rest of the lecture. She understood what he said but she didn't entirely agree with it in this case.

"What you did was potentially very dangerous. You took your friends—your team—into a situation that you didn't have all the intel about. You ignored and went against your superiors." He shook his head. "It's my fault. I should have taught you better."

"It's not your fault, Agent Connor." Cameron stepped forward. "We understood what we were doing."

"In the future, please at least try to keep me in the loop." The agent turned and took hold of the door handle. "I am your ally, Raine. I'm here to help."

Mara dropped the ring onto her desk and sighed. "It's him." She looked at Xander. "Our worst-case scenario."

Xander gently held Mara. "We beat him once, we can do it again." He squeezed her shoulder. "Now we know who it is, we have a better idea of his plans and methods."

"Gunnar never was an easy foe." Mara gave Xander a weak smile. "You're right, of course."

"Now we need to find out what his plan is." Xander stepped away. "I will speak to my contacts and see if they have any ideas on what he has been doing and might be planning."

"I will ask around too." Mara sat behind her desk. "No other students will be harmed. Especially by him."

***

"How did it go with the headmistress?" Philip handed Raine a Snickers bar as they settled into the window seat. "Your thunderous expressions say it wasn't great."

Raine sighed. "They're grounding us. They don't want us to go anywhere near the passages anymore, and we're not allowed anywhere but classes, library, dining hall, and our room." Raine bit into her Snickers bar. "I think they're too wrapped up in their own pasts. The headmistress was terrified when she saw that ring, which means it's from someone she knows. Students are being hurt and I won't sit back and allow that to continue. We can come at this from a fresh new angle."

Cameron put his arm around her shoulders. He liked seeing her fire and determination.

"This means we'll have to be sneakier." Evie offered her M&Ms to Sara. "What about Librarian Decker?"

"I think he's still a good ally." Cameron rested his head on the top of Raine's. "We didn't mention his name and he's been really cool so far."

"I agree with Cameron. We'll have to be really careful how we talk about it, but I think he's still on our side." Raine sighed. "Agent Connor gave me a lecture about respecting my superiors. He wasn't wrong. If that had been a real case, I'd have screwed up so badly. This isn't, though, and I really think the headmistress and Professor Powell mean well, but they're too busy and worried about whoever this person is to take actions we can."

"We'll need to up our game if we take on someone that scary." Evie pulled out her notebook. "I have a few potions Professor Fowler taught me after classes. I think they could be useful."

"We'll have to be careful how we approach Professor Powell's extra classes." Adrien ate one of his Doritos. "We don't want to tip him off that we're still going after this thing."

"Do you think some info about that thief will be in the books?" Cameron squeezed Raine's shoulders, knowing how much she loved books. "His ring was very distinctive."

Raine thought for a long moment. She had a good idea of how it looked in her mind.

"Perhaps. There's a small section in the library for old covens, brotherhoods, and so on." She took another bite of her Snickers. "I suspect that it'll be hidden away in the professors' library, though."

"Does this mean we're breaking into their library?" William grinned and felt a thrill run through him. He'd been dying to know what they hid in there. "I'm pretty good at picking locks."

"I think we'll have to lay low for a few days at least." Raine leaned into Cameron. "I'm not sure how closely they'll watch us. I might not even be able to look through the right books in the library."

"We can plan a library break-in quietly." Cameron

looked around to make sure no one was listening. "That'll look like we're only hanging out."

"A few days of thinking and planning shouldn't be the end of the world." Evie squeezed Raine's hand. "I get that you're frustrated, but we'll solve this."

"I hate the feeling that I screwed up. I'm trying to do the right thing, but maybe my methods weren't perfect." Raine sighed. "I really hope my uncle isn't upset with me for doing this. I'm doing everything I can to be a good agent, and sometimes, that means taking risks."

Cameron kissed her temple. "I'm sure he'll understand."

"You always put other people first." Sara reached over and squeezed Raine's arm. "He'll get it. And hey, we all make mistakes sometimes."

Raine smiled and relaxed. She hadn't followed true agent protocol, but she would at least try to keep the head-mistress and Agent Connor in the loop from there on out.

"So, what's step one?" William grinned. "Will we try the books? Or sneak around to find some new passages and rooms to check?"

Raine laughed. She was lucky to have such good friends.

"I think today and tomorrow we stick here and do normal student things." She allowed herself to relax. "They'll watch us really closely, so we can't risk anything. Who's heard the new Kaleo album?"

Raine had been right. They had seen the teachers stop by and check on the students far more than usual for the next couple of days. The group had studiously kept their conversations to perfectly innocent things. At least while someone else was in earshot.

CHAPTER TWENTY-FIVE

The professors began to think that Raine and her friends had given up on their quest to find the artifact. Raine, however, had worked with the head librarian to sneak blueprints into her room so they could plot their next move. The hounds had grown bolder once more. Raine heard the telltale clicking of nails along the hallway outside her door. The other students were locked away in their rooms. The teachers had given strict instructions not to engage with the canines.

Raine ignored that instruction. She wouldn't sit and do nothing when she could help people. It was still early, and Christie was at orchestra practice. The doors were all safely closed with extra wards on them to protect the students' minds and bodies. Thus far, the hounds had only walked the hallways and rooms where the wards were less secure.

The hound paused outside the door as she approached it with her wand raised. Evie and Sara were behind her.

Evie had a vial of what could only be described as goo in her hand. It had been designed to cling to the hound and hopefully make it impossible for it to vanish on them. They then planned to banish it fully. If it worked, Evie would make more potions and they'd work their way through the hound population. "Please let there only be a few of these hounds," Raine whispered and held her wand steady. It was a slow method, but they'd take whatever worked.

She yanked the door open and threw a stun spell at the hound. The animal froze mid-lunge but it squirmed and fought against her spell. Evie whispered the appropriate words and launched her vial at the hound at the moment it broke through.

The canine stopped and dripped with luminous green and purple goo. It bared its teeth and stalked slowly toward them.

"I thought it was supposed to stop dead." Sara raised her chin. "Because it's moving pretty well."

"Try the dispelling." Raine formed the visualization in her mind. "Now."

The trio had practiced all night. They spoke the words as one and their magic wove together and struck the hound square in the chest. It was supposed to vanish and leave nothing but the goo behind. Instead, it grew bigger.

"What did we do wrong!?" Sara stepped back. "We were so sure."

Raine pushed her friends back inside the room and slammed the door shut. "Where did we get that spell from?" She frowned and tried to remember. "Was it in that weird book?"

"Yeah." Evie rushed forward and pulled it out from under her bed. "This one."

Raine had been so pleased to see the book she hadn't given it too much thought. Now, she inspected it closely. There was no library stamp. No library barcode. Nothing. It was merely a thin, musty old book.

"You found this in the library?" She began to think they'd been set up. "It doesn't have any library markers on it."

"No. It was on the bookshelf at the back of Professor Hudson's classroom." Evie sighed and flopped on her bed as the hound bayed outside. "We were played, weren't we?"

"I think so." Raine dropped the book on the cabinet next to her bed. "It looks like a real book, but it wouldn't have been too difficult to change the title of that spell."

"I'm sorry." Evie looked down. "I should have known it was too good to be true."

Raine went to her and hugged her. "Don't be ridiculous. None of us really know this type of spell and they took advantage of that." Raine scooted over to let Sara hug Evie too. "We'll be more careful next time."

***

No one was bitten that night, but there were a few close calls. Professor Grant had saved a freshman who had panicked and frozen when a hound attacked him. The professor had summoned a huge explosive spell that she targeted at the beast's heart. It exploded and small specks of ash showered the student.

Mara fielded phone calls from worried parents all

morning. She dragged her fingers through her hair and sighed. While she understood their concerns, she was doing everything she could. They tried to track down the artifact and Gunnar, but it was slow going. They leaned on all their contacts, but they didn't have much spare time. Between teaching, the accompanying paperwork, and dealing with concerned parents, Mara hadn't been able to achieve as much as she wanted.

"I understand Mr. Fitz. We are doing everything within our power to keep the students safe. I know that you're worried, and that is very valid. Your son will not be harmed."

Mr. Fitz remained silent for a full minute. Mara was about to check if he was still on the line when he said, "Okay. Fine."

He hung up and left her feeling frazzled and exhausted. She'd been through many similar conversations. The phone rang again with the next one.

"The holidays are soon. Are they canceling the ball?" Sara took a mouthful of her lasagna. "I heard they're thinking about letting us have small parties in our rooms and the classrooms."

"We could have one in our movie room." William finished his garlic bread. "Something small and fun."

"I like that idea." Adrien pushed his empty plate away. "Do you think we can get the stuff together in time, Philip?"

"We can go down to the kemana tomorrow." Philip finished his water. "Get some decorations and candy."

"Oh, we need candy apples." Evie's eyes lit up. "They're so good and I've never managed to make them quite right."

"Will they let us go down to the kemana?" Cameron chewed on the end of his pen. He tried to work on his essay while eating dinner. "Aren't we still grounded?"

"Everyone's allowed to go down into the kemana for two hours tomorrow." Raine looked on with delight when a slice of pumpkin pie appeared in front of her. "To prepare for Halloween."

"I think we're supposed to be chaperoned." Sara wrinkled her nose in disdain. "That'll kill some of the fun."

"You'll be accompanied by me." Agent Connor smiled at the group. "I hope that won't kill your fun too badly. Your headmistress has given me the necessary background about the kemana. I understand it's a rare privilege for a human to go down there."

"I'm sure it'll be great." Raine smiled at him, not wanting to offend him. "Thanks for taking the time out of your day."

"It's not a worry. I'll get things for the teachers' party." The agent turned away. "Does eleven work for you?"

"Perfect." Raine picked up her fork. "Thanks again."

"He seems kind of cool." Cameron took a large bite out of his pumpkin pie. "I didn't picture the teachers having a Halloween party, though."

"I don't know." Evie shrugged. "I think Professor Grant really knows how to dance and she looks like she'd be the life of the party."

"I bet Professor Powell would surprise you too." Sara gestured with her fork. "I bet he makes a mean cocktail."

"I want to see this party now." Evie laughed. "It'd be so weird seeing the teachers away from their usual environment. Am I ready for that?"

"I don't think any of us are." Adrien laughed. "It's probably best we stick to our own party."

CHAPTER TWENTY-SIX

Raine looked at the spellbook Librarian Decker had loaned her. It was full of Halloween decoration spells. She hadn't thought that such books existed, but it was useful. This was her third attempt to form fake spider webs to hang from the corners. The first time, they had fallen in limp strings into a heap on the floor. The second time, they'd looked more like grey mush.

Adrien came over to see if he could help her understand where she went wrong.

"How're you visualizing the webs?" He looked at the spell. "You need to view them as full webs rather than the weird almost mesh-like webs they tend to use for Halloween decorations."

Raine raised her wand once more. "I pictured the Halloween decoration style ones." She grinned at him. "Thanks!"

The spell worked perfectly that time. The corners and edges of the room were soon covered in hanging cobwebs. Sara had hung small pumpkins from the ceiling. They glowed with little fireballs and cast an orange light over the room. Evie had cast a spell on the floor that made it look like they were stood over an endless chasm or pit.

Philip set out the sodas and candies on the fold-up table. They'd picked out a large range of things to suit everyone's tastes and desires throughout the night. The teachers had pushed lights-out to midnight, so everyone had time to relax and enjoy the evening. They had worked tirelessly all day to ensure the students would be safe while the veil was thinner.

No one had seen or heard the hounds for a couple of nights and an air of hope ran through the school. Raine wasn't convinced. She had researched every possible spell and potion they could use against the hounds. The problem was that she couldn't find what the hounds were made from. If she didn't know what they were made of she didn't know which spell type to focus on.

Cameron wrapped his arms around her waist and leaned around to kiss her cheek from behind.

"Are you ready for our adventure later?" He rested his head against hers and enjoyed being close to her. "I have everything set up and covered."

"Yeah. I have the spells memorized, Evie's stashed the potions under the refreshment table, and Adrien has an extra dagger for you if you want it." She rested her hands on his. "We're doing the right thing. I know Agent Connor will lecture me again, but there's a risk the thief will only escalate things. We need to make sure no one gets seriously hurt."

"You don't have to convince me." Cameron released her

to stand by her side. "I won't sit idly by when we could do something to help. Agent Connor will understand."

William started the music and familiar modern rock filled the room. Sara threw her hands up and danced while she continued to weave the spell that added small skeleton paintings to the walls. Bats fluttered between the hanging pumpkins and Philip added a bubbling cauldron to the far corner. Pale silver smoke rolled off the cauldron and it looked incredibly real. He beamed with pride. It had taken him three days to perfect that illusion spell.

"This looks amazing." Raine looked around the room. "Remember, lights are supposed to be out by midnight. And none of us walk around the school alone."

"I love this song!" Evie took William's hand and pulled him to the middle of the movie room where she started to dance. "It has such an amazing beat."

William was completely lost and didn't know how to dance. He tried to move his body with the beat and hoped he didn't look like too much of a dork. Raine and Cameron were near the refreshments table eating candy corn and debating what the best flavor of Oreos was.

"You can't go wrong with the classic." Cameron put another candy in his mouth. "It's the classic for a reason."

"Those mint ones, though." Raine grinned. "They're so addictive."

"Nothing beats those special edition Peeps ones." Adrien took some candy corn. "Now they were addictive."

"I never tried them." Cameron sighed melodramatically. "Maybe they'll bring them back at some point."

The clock chimed eight o'clock and the atmosphere changed. They'd had two hours to party, and this was the time to sneak out and begin their exploration again. The blueprints showed there was a passageway some eight feet outside the movie room. Cameron had investigated and was confident he could open the entrance to it. Then, they'd move quickly down the passage into the basement-level room that fit the bill for a ritual room perfectly. It was completely round, had no windows, and had a weird symbol on it.

Philip looked around the door and made sure the hall outside the movie room was clear. He stepped out with Adrien directly behind him. Something moved ahead and he instinctively pulled back into the room, thinking it could be a teacher. It wasn't quite right, though. He frowned and looked at it more closely.

Raine stepped forward to see what had caught his attention. The being moved toward them and could only be described as a wraith. It stood at almost seven feet tall and eerie black smoke drifted around it. Orange eyes glowed like lit embers from the darkness where its head should have been. Long talons tipped its skeletal fingers and sharp yellow teeth were the only indication of a mouth.

Cameron moved beside Raine on one side and William to the other. Raine and William both had the same thought and formed light spells. They threw the spells simultaneously at the wraith. It paused for a moment before it vanished and reappeared directly in front of them.

Cameron snarled and leapt on the wraith. He intended to tear into it but his hands went through to the cool air beyond it. There was a light resistance but nothing he could work with.

The others cycled through air and fire spells in search of some way to disperse the specter. Cameron worked to distract it and continued to claw at it in an effort to pull chunks away from the main body. It provided enough interference for the group to fire an explosive water spell at it. The wraith screamed before it turned into a black pool on the floor and the entity disappeared. Cameron turned to make sure that Raine and his friends were okay.

"I don't think the water really worked against it." Raine nudged the black pool with her toe. "I think the thief grew bored and made it vanish."

"Or wanted to make us think it worked." William crouched down to look at the black water. "So that next time we see one, we try water and fail."

"Do we give up looking for the entrance already?" Raine looked around and listened for any new disturbances.

"We're running out of time. We'll be missed if we stay much longer. We'll have to come back another time." William started to head back and the others followed reluctantly. Another time, they would find the secrets the building still held.

CHAPTER TWENTY-SEVEN

"Did you hear those wraith things almost got into Jack's room last night?" Evie handed William the popcorn to pop. "There were claw marks on the door in the morning."

"Well, that tells us they can become physical." Raine curled up beside Cameron. "The professors having us locked down really derails our plans."

"It took a lot of planning to figure out how to still have a movie night." Philip poured a cream soda. "I get it, but it's really frustrating. If we could only get into those secret passages, I'm sure we could make some progress."

"We're within eight feet of the entrance, according to the blueprint. This seems like a good time to keep going." William straightened as he grew more excited. "There are no professors to stop us."

"There's always someone watching us, especially these days." Raine had learned from Agent Connor. Follow the rules and still search for the solution. Both were possible.

William rolled his eyes in frustration.

"Of course, the more time they spend locking us down, the less time they put into finding the thief." Raine sighed and leaned into Cameron. "I understand, I really do. The parents have also made life very difficult. And I get that too, but I want to wrap this up before someone gets badly hurt."

Cameron stroked Raine's arm. "We'll do it. We're getting closer. The professors move in patterns, so if we time it right, we'll be able to get an hour to explore soon." He smiled. "Are we watching *Invasion of the Body Snatchers* today?"

"Yes!" Sara grinned and took her popcorn from William. "Thanks. I'd be lost without my popcorn."

He smiled and settled down on the couch.

"Is this one of the black and white ones?" Adrien took a sip of his cream soda. "I'm growing fond of those really old ones."

"Oh, wow, look at her dress!" Sara pointed at the woman on the screen. "Is that her daily dress? It's so glamorous and beautiful."

"They really did dress differently back then." Raine bit into her Twizzler. "I can't say I'd want to wear that every day, though. It's not practical enough for me."

"True, not every day." Sara shrugged. "But sometimes, it's nice to dress up for the day, even if you only go to the grocery store."

They watched in silence for a moment.

"If I start saying something weird like Adrien is possessed, I hope you believe me." Sara put a handful of popcorn into her mouth. "So many movies start with someone saying what has happened and no one believes them."

"I'm sure there's societal commentary to be made there." Philip shrugged and ate some popcorn. "I don't want to think too hard tonight, though."

"Oh, my word, I couldn't use one of those push lawn mowers." Evie pulled out another Twizzler. "They look like so much work. I don't mind putting in some elbow grease, but they look like too much."

"I'm not a fan of gardening to begin with." Adrien stretched. "I'd definitely avoid one of those."

"I like the look of those old English country gardens but not the amount of work that goes into them." Evie shook her head. "I'd have to be rich and hire someone else to do it for me."

"I'd rather have my house back onto the forest." Adrien frowned at the tv. "No upkeep, pretty, and entirely natural."

"As long as no bears came visiting." Sara grinned. "Do they even have bears in France?"

"There's a tiny population around the mountains but nothing anyone would notice." Adrien ate some of his popcorn. "I like the idea of stepping out of my back door and walking into the peaceful forest."

Something shifted in the corner of the movie room. The shadow flickered and deepened. Adrien felt the magic before he saw the details of it. His focus on the shadow drew Raine's attention, and quickly, Cameron's. They watched as the shadow transformed into a wraith.

The group pushed to their feet in readiness within a couple of seconds. The entity simply stood and watched them for a long minute. Raine couldn't shake the feeling it was playing with them.

Evie slipped a bright blue vial from her pocket and threw it at the wraith. She'd done her research and felt good about the cage potion she'd thrown. It was designed to ground anything incorporeal in the physical world and bind it to where it stood. The shadow screeched and thrashed. The music from the movie took on a distinctly alarmed tone which seemed ironically appropriate.

Finally, the entity stopped screeching and froze in place. The students approached and circled around it, their magic at the ready with spells on the tips of their tongues. Cameron poked at it and found it to be entirely solid. His wolf instincts told him to tear it apart and keep his friends safe.

"Adrien, can you feel its magic?" Raine looked at the elf. "Can you tell us what type of magic has formed it?"

Adrien closed his eyes. He hadn't had much training on this particular type of tracking. His mother was an expert at it, but thus far, he hadn't shown a great deal of potential. He stretched his magic and looked closely at the wraith through the lens of his enchantment. Dark-grey threads stretched upward from it like strings on a puppet, but he couldn't follow them beyond the ceiling of the room.

The wraith began to turn translucent and Raine felt their time slip through her fingertips.

"We need to figure out where it's come from and how to stop it." She gripped her wand tighter. "Does anyone have any spells for that?"

"We'd have to magically dissect it, and even then, I don't

think we know enough." Evie ground her teeth. "I don't even know what to research."

The wraith vanished and left splotches of blue on the floor.

"We know we can make it physical." Cameron put his hands on Raine's shoulders which calmed her. "That means we can kill it."

Raine nodded and relaxed. She had grown frustrated at their lack of progress. They hadn't found anything on the ring emblem. Even though they'd explored every relevant inch of the library, they came up blank.

"We need to get into the professors' library." Raine looked at William. "Do you think you can get us in?"

"I can do it." William gave a firm nod. "We should do it now."

The quiet halls had an eerie quality. They were usually full of laughter and conversations but now, they were entirely empty. It acted to harden Raine's resolve to find the artifact thief and end the reign of fear over the school. Every door was closed with a small rune carved into it to protect those inside. Some of the runes were frayed around the edges where wraiths or hounds had tried to get in.

Nails clicked somewhere above them. Everyone tensed in preparation and formed explosive light spells in their mind. They weren't perfect but they did at least drive the hounds off for a time. They remained in a tight group and watched every angle as they approached the professors' library. They hadn't seen a single soul on their little journey. If a professor saw them, they'd be in deep trouble.

Raine's instincts said to use stealth spells but that might not help. There was a chance the professors would see through them. She made a note to ask Librarian Decker about learning better, stronger stealth spells. They were something that could be very useful when she was an agent.

William crouched in front of the lock to the professors' library and set to work. It was complicated and heavily warded. He slowed his breathing and focused entirely on each layer of the lock until it seemed there was nothing in the world but those layers of magic.

The half-Ifrit pressed his magic gently against the first layer and felt for the relevant threads. The key was to bend the threads carefully away without breaking them. If they broke, the wards would be activated, and the professors would come running. The first two layers weren't too difficult and he had slipped into a familiar groove when he reached the second to last layer.

Those remaining were far more complicated. Rather than being akin to spider webs with clear threads and lines he could work with, they were more like a mesh. William was sure that he could work his way through them but he needed to remain calm.

A cold breeze pooled around his feet and ran down his spine. Raine whispered something and a tightness spread over him. He had been hidden inside a shield. William tried to work more quickly, all too aware that his friends fought something off. He thought it was a wraith, but he needed to focus entirely on the mesh and couldn't be distracted even for the second it would take to confirm it.

The shield lifted, and he was down to the final layer. A hand squeezed his shoulder gently. The comfort and security that came from Evie's touch gave him the clarity he needed to bend the final four threads in the right way. The lock clicked open and he stood with a sense of triumph. William opened the door and a loud sound burst forth.

The group ran as fast as they could to the safety of their movie room before the professors could catch them. Raine suspected that she and her group of friends would be at the top of the list of culprits, but if they could reach their movie room in time, they'd be safe and clear.

They dropped down onto the couch just as the finale of the movie started. Raine still hadn't quite caught her breath when Professor Hudson flung the door open. Their movie room had been discovered. They all jumped and turned to face her. Better to be caught watching movies than breaking into the professors' library.

Professor Hudson narrowed her eyes at the group, looking around the room. "Rules have been made for a reason." Her voice was cool and even. "If you want to use this room again, you'll need permission and an escort from a professor."

She seemed unaware of how fast all their hearts were beating. They had cut it really close that time.

CHAPTER TWENTY-EIGHT

Professor Fowler took another vitality potion before the students started coming into her class. She had spent most of the night brewing potions to help protect the school and its students. She'd worked with the pixies to add something into everyone's food to keep them safe. There wasn't anything to keep them entirely safe, but it would boost their immune systems and help them sleep a little better. Many had reported being haunted through their dreams.

"Today, you will brew a potion to defend against nightmares." Professor Fowler put on her best smile. "It is something that you have full permission to make for yourselves should you need to."

With the number of students suffering as they had it was decided that all relevant classes would be turned toward protection and defense against the hounds and wraiths.

"The key to this potion is the quality of the ingredients. You will be given access to every ingredient you need, even outside of classroom hours. They are of the highest quality and will be entirely free to every student." She placed the recipe card down on each desk. "You should aim for a red licorice tasting and colored potion. It should be slightly thicker than water and have a soft sweetness to it."

A Wood Elf raised his hand.

"I hate licorice. Can we make it another flavor?"

Professor Fowler smiled. She was asked that same question every year that she taught this potion.

"Yes. If you read your recipe card you will see there are several flavors you can add to the potion. Please do not stray from that list. Doing so will adversely affect the potion."

Raine looked at the recipe card and was pleased to see that lemon sherbet was on the list of possible flavors. She liked red licorice but not dark licorice. She'd stomach it if she had to, but she'd rather not. Lemon, however, was something she loved.

"If you make this potion for your friends, be aware that shifters need a higher dose. You are also not permitted to sell it." She looked sternly at Philip. "Begin when you're ready."

Raine read the recipe twice before she picked up the licorice leaf and valerian root. She crushed the root and added the leaf in a slow, methodical manner. Evie moved quickly through the recipe, a speed she had developed through experience. Raine, however, was still being very careful and made sure that everything was perfect. Cameron had suffered quietly from nightmares and she wanted to ease his sleep.

Once the root and leaf had been thoroughly crushed

together, she added them to the icy cold water in the small cauldron before her. The rest of the classroom faded out of focus as she moved through the steps on the recipe. There was something increasingly soothing about potion making. She could see why Evie enjoyed it so much.

The recipe called for eight minutes and four seconds of steady stirring before she could add the crushed acorn to it. The time ticked by slowly and gave her time to consider their next move. It was difficult to get into the hidden passageways, but they had made their way through every room in the school. The thief was within the building somewhere and caused increasing pain and grief. Raine needed it to stop.

Once the time was up, she added the acorn and stirred in a figure-of-eight pattern before adding the marigold petals, sea salt, and sage leaves. The potion began to thicken into a deep, rich purple liquid. She continued to stir and added her magic slowly into the mix. The color deepened, and she felt as though it was something she could give to Cameron. She hated seeing the shadows under his eyes and knowing that he was struggling. He remained bright and supportive, but it still worried her. It wasn't in her nature to stand by and watch her friends suffer.

Evie leaned over and looked at Raine's potion. "That looks amazing!" She beamed at Raine. "You've come so far. I'm really proud of you."

"Do you think it's good enough to give to Cameron?" Raine continued to stir slowly. "He's had nightmares recently."

"It looks it to me. There should be enough there for a

week's supply." Evie poured her own potion into the beaker. "He can have mine too."

None of the girls had suffered from nightmares thus far. Raine put it down to the runes and wards they had put around their room. They had devoted the whole weekend to the process and applied everything Professor Powell had taught them. The boys hadn't been quite so dedicated and suffered for it.

Professor Fowler walked around the room and was relieved to see that everyone had made their potion right.

"You're all free to take these tonight as you need." The professor smiled. "Use the last fifteen minutes of the class to catch up on any homework you might have."

She had made a large batch of the nightmare protection potion for the other professors. They had been hit particularly hard. Whatever was in the school was very talented and had worked its way through the professors' wards and protections. No one had been seriously hurt yet, but it was only a matter of time.

Gunnar looked out the window over the frost-covered grounds and smiled when he felt the low hum of fear fill his veins. His magic grew stronger by the day. The wraiths had been a stroke of genius. They had taken the fear to a whole new level which had helped his magic grow far quicker than expected.

The students that had tried to track him had been held back by their professors' desires and attempts to protect them. That had given him more time and space to continue with his plan at a leisurely pace. He wasn't in a rush. The school was quite comfortable. He had successfully crept into the kitchens for some of the best food he'd had in years, and the room he had chosen to occupy had come with old furniture. He congratulated himself on a job well done.

CHAPTER TWENTY-NINE

"Leigh went to the nurse's office earlier." Cameron leaned closer so no one could hear what he said. "She was the one we spoke to at the art show with the mark."

"Is she okay?" Raine moved away from the other students. "Was it the mark?"

"I heard she's fallen into a coma." Cameron hugged her gently at the thought of losing her. "Rumors say that the mark had spread across most of her body."

Raine swallowed hard. "From what I remember, the hounds bite anyone with a secret. Their bites are poison, and that poison slowly consumes you. The bigger the secret, the more painful and quick-acting the poison." She shook her head. "I guess her secret wasn't that big."

Cameron closed his eyes and sighed. "What are we going to do now?" He motioned Evie and William over. "This is escalating."

"We need to get into that professors' library and the hidden passages." Raine ran her fingers through his hair in an effort to soothe him. "We start with the library as it's likely to have something to help us."

"I'm not sure I can get through the extra locks." William frowned. "I already triggered the wards once."

"I believe in you." Raine smiled at him. "I'm sure you can do it. You know the wards are there now."

Evie put her arm around William. "We'll be right there with you. I can help you with the wards." She gave him a devilish smile. "I broke into my father's office a few times. I'm pretty good with security wards."

William nodded. He wasn't going to be able to get out of this without agreeing to it. He wanted to help, but he wasn't sure that he could pull off what they asked of him.

"We'll try it tonight." Raine nodded. "First, we go and get dinner."

She walked with Cameron at her side and tried to act as though everything was completely normal. They couldn't let on that they plotted how to get into the professors' library so they could save the school from a dark wizard.

"Sara and Philip, act as lookouts. Evie and William, handle the actual lock. Cameron and I will work with Adrien to cover the security aspect." Raine looked at her friends. "Everyone okay with that?"

They nodded. There was a thrill of excitement at the fact they were breaking into the professors' library. Raine hesitated and her heart pounded as Agent Connor's voice echoed in her thoughts. She shook her head and pressed her eyes closed for a moment. *Sometimes, there's a good reason for breaking a rule. At least, I hope there is.*

They wandered along the hall as though they were simply looking for a nice spot to hang out for a little while. It was already lights-out but it wasn't that unusual for students to sneak out for an hour to catch up on gossip or spend some time with their partners.

"I can't believe you cheated on me."

"You're so ridiculously high maintenance. I can't believe you blame me."

"How am I high maintenance? And you're supposed to apologize, not blame me."

"You insist on presents for every absurd little anniversary and we've only been together for three months."

"That is not high maintenance. I simply believe in celebrating the milestones."

"Demanding a piece of jewelry for the month anniversary of our first kiss is ridiculous."

A Light Elf girl stormed past them and Raine fought to keep a straight face.

"I'd never cheat on you." Cameron kissed Raine's cheek. "And you're definitely not high maintenance."

"I'm not sure when our anniversary is—is that a problem?" Raine glanced at him. "I didn't really think to write it down in my calendar."

Cameron laughed. "Don't worry, I did note it down." He squeezed Raine closer. "It's things like that that makes me like you."

Raine shook her head and laughed. He was so genuine that she wouldn't argue with him.

They reached the professors' library and Adrien stood

beside them with his sword drawn. They weren't sure how much good it would do against the hounds, but they would try.

William crouched in front of the lock and began work. Evie stood near him with her wand raised. She was ready to break through the wards. She enjoyed watching William work with the way his face scrunched up in concentration. He was the most adorable guy she'd ever met and she hoped they spent many long and happy years together.

Raine itched to get moving. She hated having to wait while William broke into the library. It wasn't in her nature to stand by and watch as other people did the work. She calmed herself and drew on her martial arts training to find inner peace and work through her impatience and frustration. There would be plenty of times when she had to remain still and quiet as an agent. If nothing else, there would be stakeouts.

Evie moved into place to work her way through the wards. She called her magic and pressed it gently into the wards as the locks clicked and William opened the door. The wards were far more complicated than those her father had used. That wouldn't stop Evie, though. They were taunted by the artifact thief. An innocent girl was in a coma thanks to him. Evie was determined to get into that room and find the information they needed.

Raine felt as though they had stood there for hours when they finally heard the signal to move into the library. She and the others rushed inside and Evie closed the door with a quiet snick behind them. She had set the wards in such a way that they'd be able to get back out again without any trouble.

Unlike the main library downstairs, there weren't nice, easy signs to guide them to the section they needed. Raine appreciated that, though, as it gave her an excuse to wander through the space and explore the books they had chosen to hide in there. The group split up and each student explored a section. They hunted for something on the secrets the school held.

Cameron remained close to Raine. Something about the library set his teeth on edge. He'd heard that some of those books contained dark magic and didn't want Raine to be pulled into something dangerous like that. The shifter studied the shelves and hunted for keywords such as school, Turner Underwood, and hidden rooms. He found books on mysterious animals, rituals, blood magic, and something about cooking for the dark side.

Raine had a fantastic time looking through everything. There were so many titles she was dying to pull out and read through, but she knew their time was limited. They needed to make sure they only took the relevant book.

Evie called out. "I have something over here."

The group converged on her section which was filled with topics on hidden everything from rooms, beings, and magic forms, through to artifacts and herbs. They each took a shelf and finally, Philip found the book they knew had to be in there somewhere. It was a slender book with dark brown leather binding and gold lettering.

"The hidden rooms of the Underwood mansion."

Philip handed the book to Raine who slipped it into her satchel and they left the room. William and Evie worked to restore everything as it needed to be. Someone was coming up the stairs when they strolled casually back toward their

dorm rooms. They decided it would look far more suspicious if they ran there.

<hr>

Gunnar stepped into the shadows where the students couldn't see him. He paused and held still as he watched them pass, a look of bemusement on his face. They had no idea how close they were to their foe.

CHAPTER THIRTY

Dorvu took to the skies when he heard the hounds in the woods again. He was sick and tired of those interlopers on his grounds. He had heard that they'd hurt some students and that only angered him further. The dragon flew in low circles and waited for the hounds to emerge. He was determined to do everything he could to keep the students safe.

Just when he grew bored, a pack of hounds accompanied by a wraith hurtled out of the woods. The dragon swooped down and tried to pick one up with his claws. It turned incorporeal before his claws could make contact with it. Dorvu huffed out a blast of icy cold air at them in frustration. That slowed some of them down, at least.

Grinning to himself, Dorvu began to breathe long streams of icy air over the hounds. It took two laps around the paddock but two of them finally became entirely physical. He landed and snapped at the hound. His jaws closed around thin air when it managed to duck away at the last second. The dragon raced after it and finally managed to bite one.

The rest of the pack turned and ran straight at Dorvu. He thought this was a fantastic game and bit and clawed his way through the pack and enjoyed that he finally made some real progress. The taste of soot and death coated his tongue, but it was a small price to pay for knowing that he had helped keep the school safe.

Horace watched from the barn as the dragon took on the pack of hounds and appeared to be winning. Many of them went up in small puffs of smoke. He was about to check on the horses one last time for the night when he heard a soft whine coming from Dorvu. One of the hounds had somehow managed to get its teeth around his scales and into his flesh. The dragon latched onto the hound and shook it until it was nothing but a wisp of darkness.

The groundskeeper didn't want to risk anything and ran over to the dragon. Dorvu slumped onto the grass as Horace leapt over a fence. When the groundskeeper got there, he was in a deep sleep. No matter how hard Horace tried to shake him or rouse him, the dragon slept on.

The hounds were gone but they had achieved what they had set out to do.

Mara called to Lucy and Elias when Horace brought the news. They all ran across the frosty grass to the sleeping dragon.

Elias lifted Dorvu's eyelid while Lucy ran her hands over his scales.

"He's only sleeping. It's nothing more malicious than that." Elias sighed. "It was one of those hounds that did this?"

"Yes." Horace put his hands in his pockets. "I watched it happen. There was nothing I could do. He was hunting them and making good progress too."

"We're going to need a few herbs." Lucy ran the possibilities through her mind. "He'll hate the taste of it, but I know just the thing to wake him up again."

"Tell me everything you need and we'll get it." Mara frowned at the sleeping dragon. She hated seeing him like that. "Whatever it is, we'll get it."

Lucy shook her head. "Some of them are difficult to get hold of." She thought through the recipe once more. "One of them only grows in Brazil and another will need to be flown in from the Alps."

"We'll do it." Elias frowned at the dragon. "Dorvu is too important to the school."

Lucy nodded. "I'll make a list." She gave Horace a weak smile. "Don't worry, Horace, it really is only sleep. Give him shelter if the rains get heavy."

Mara walked away and felt as though the school was a little emptier without Dorvu prowling the skies overhead. She was determined to wake him as soon as possible.

They had gathered in Lucy's kitchen to see exactly what was needed for Dorvu's cure. She hadn't exaggerated when she said some of the herbs were difficult to locate. Mara took the list of the most difficult foreign ones and worked through her list of contacts. She had been around a long time and that came in very useful during moments like that.

She stepped outside and began the first phone call. "Andrew, it's Mara."

"Mara, it's been too long. To what do I owe this pleasure?"

"I need some salamander root."

"Straight to the point, I always did like that about you. And what would you need salamander root for?"

"That is my business, Andrew."

"That's a shame. I'm afraid I don't have any right now."

"I'm calling in the favor, Andrew." Mara clenched her fist. "This is that moment."

"This must be serious. I had expected you to hold out for something of higher value."

She opened the door to her own cottage. "When can you have the root to the school?"

"Two days from now. How have you been? How's Xander? Did he tell you what he used his favor on?"

Mara rolled her eyes. She was all too aware of the wedge he intended to drive between herself and Xander. She knew that Xander had chosen to use his favor to procure a dangerous dark magic artifact. What Andrew didn't know was that he had used that artifact to save thirty non-magical people.

"Goodbye, Andrew."

She hung up the phone and went into the kitchen to brew herself a nice calming tea. Andrew had always had a way to get under her skin and irritate her. She remembered the first time she'd met him. He had been a transfer to her college. They'd literally bumped into each other in the hallway. Books went flying but Andrew had made no attempt to pick his up. Instead, he'd looked far too closely at Mara. Things had only gone downhill from there.

Xander let himself into her cottage and removed his shoes. "How was Andrew?"

"Himself." She poured the hot water over the loose-leaf tea. "He tried to use the information on how you used your favor to get under my skin."

Xander laughed. "He never changes."

"Did you get anywhere with Michael?" She turned to look at him. "Does he have the herbs we need?"

"I'm taking the underground train to Mexico City Friday night. I'll be back with the herbs on Saturday afternoon." Xander pulled a mug out of the cupboard and set about making himself tea. "Lucy has secured the relevant stones."

Mara breathed a sigh of relief. Dorvu should be back to himself within a week. She hoped that he wouldn't lose too much weight during his sleep. Shaking her head, she pushed the concern aside. One week wouldn't be too bad. The dragon would fly around and hunt pheasants and rabbits before they knew it.

CHAPTER THIRTY-ONE

Xander had packed light. He would only be away for one night so there was no need to take anything more than the bare basics. He had checked on Dorvu earlier in the day and he still slept deeply with no signs of distress. Xander got into his car and began the drive to the nearest Starbucks and the hidden train platform.

He glanced backward at Dorvu and reminded himself that he was doing it for him. One of the herbs they needed for the cure was down in Mexico, and it would take too long to have it shipped to the school. Xander had made all the arrangements and it was only a matter of collecting the herbs now.

Lucy had given Mara a long list of herbs to try to find while she gathered those that were closer at hand. Mara had to drive over to Richmond, just down the highway from Charlottesville. There was an herbalist along Cary

Street next to the old Byrd Theater, hiding under the guise of a florist, as was surprisingly common. Lucy had insisted that no one else could retrieve those particular herbs. Everyone else did their part with the protections and Dorvu's cure.

Mara didn't argue. She got into her car and turned the rock station on as she settled in for the drive. She didn't much like driving around Richmond, but the dragon was an important member of the school. A little traffic was a very small price to pay to make sure that he was safe and well.

She reached the small storefront with a hand-painted sign, Vogue Florists, above the window, pulled her car around the corner, and parked along the street.

The florist was beautifully pristine and arranged inside. Elaborate bouquets had been displayed behind the tall glass counter. Flowers in every shape, size, and color were neatly set out throughout the main body of the shop so that people could create their own bouquets.

Mara looked around the flowers while she waited for another customer to complete their purchase. Once they were safely out of earshot, she smiled at the older brunette behind the counter.

"I'm here to speak to Ezra."

The brunette nodded. "Lucy said you'd be coming over. Come on."

Mara followed the woman around the counter through to the back room. The space was immaculate. Everything clearly had a place, and everything was where it belonged. Dried herbs hung from evenly spaced hooks on the ceiling and vials were arranged along the back wall. All were empty and ready to be filled with dried herbs or potions.

Ezra turned out to be a twenty-something red-haired man with a brilliant smile and emerald green eyes.

"Mara, it's a pleasure to meet you. I'll have the herbs for you in a moment."

He turned his back and proceeded to package the herbs into a neat sky-blue box. She noted that each herb went into its own section within the larger box. Mara loved the organization and wished more people would embrace that. Xander was awful for throwing things everywhere and living in a state of perpetual chaos. He knew where everything was but no one else did. Of course, Mara suspected that was the entire purpose.

"Everything you need is in here. Payment has been covered. Do have a good journey back."

Ezra handed the box to her before he returned to his herbs on the redwood desk in the middle of the room. Mara appreciated the lack of small talk and the pure efficiency of the exchange. She turned and headed back to her car.

Xander really missed the fresh, crisp air of Virginia as he walked down the streets of Mexico City. His contact wasn't too far away but he had chosen a small shop off the main streets. To Xander's dismay, that meant there would be no air conditioning. He kept his wand close as he watched the way some of the locals looked at him. It had been a long time since he had been in Mexico City. His name wasn't really known around there which was both a good and a bad thing. It really depended on the situation.

The contact sat inside a small run-down café, waiting for him. The cafe was empty with only an older woman behind the counter at the back who cleaned and looked away studiously. Xander rolled his eyes. He hated such theatrics. The herb he was there for was rare, but it wasn't that valuable.

He sat down opposite the middle-aged man and said nothing but simply waited for him to place the herb on the table. The man took his time which made Xander literally sweat. He finally placed the slender yellow stem onto the table. The professor handed the cash over, got up, and left. The transaction was complete and he was free to return to the blissfully cool safety of the magical trains underground. He could even stop for coffee as he passed through the Starbucks. Cold coffee, of course.

At least he had the herb for Dorvu. The dragon would fly around the grounds again in no time. Xander was sure the rabbits and pheasants had enjoyed the respite, but everyone had missed the silver dragon's presence. He had become a key part of the school atmosphere.

CHAPTER THIRTY-TWO

Gunnar sat in his favorite chair and looked out at the night sky. His hounds terrorized the school and sent sweet, delicious fear into the simple black cube next to him. The cube turned that fear into powerful magic that filled his veins. Mara and Xander had been too foolish and hadn't realized the scale of his plans.

The second cube had taken him a long time to procure but it had been worth every second of planning and the agony he'd endured. When he had first heard about it, he had thought it to be nothing more than an idle myth. Surely no one would have truly made an artifact that turned fear into magic?

Then he found someone who had seen the artifact and the effect it had for themselves. That was when Gunnar knew that he needed to have that cube. He had been humiliated and cast out from his own family. Revenge was the only thing that kept him going. Gunnar had resolved to show the world that he was not some weak little boy as his father asserted. He was a god among men, and he would make everyone bow down to him.

The cube had been hidden deep in the Italian countryside. The small town was far away from the usual tourist routes and that had made it more difficult for Gunnar to keep his presence hidden. It had taken many glamors and illusions to make himself look like a local. He had devoted six months to learning Italian and perfecting the local accent before he moved there. Everything had to be done so very carefully.

No one could know that it was Gunnar that had taken the cube. If they knew, the entire plan would fall apart before he could implement it. Once he had moved into the town under the guise of a painter living off his large trust fund, he set about finding the exact location of the cube. Of course, that was no easy task as he couldn't simply ask the locals. No, he needed to learn the secrets of the place and find out exactly how the town worked.

It had taken a month of getting to know everyone and learning how to manipulate them before he came across Maria. She was a beautiful woman with rich brown eyes and pitch-colored hair almost down to her waist. Maria had lost her husband two years prior and she was ready to find a new companion. Gunnar was more than happy to fill that role for her. During the long nights, Maria would tell him stories from the town.

One night, she spoke of the time a group of the older men came back into the town under the cover of darkness. They were hiding something, she knew it. Maria hated not knowing what was going on. She kept track of everyone and made sure that no one could possibly have any secrets that she didn't know about. Gunnar had been drawn to her for exactly that reason.

Maria followed the men deep into the cellar at the vineyard and watched in bemusement as they revealed a simple black cube. She couldn't understand why they would go to such effort to hide a cube like that. Of course, she didn't know about magic and couldn't know its significance. Gunnar maintained his facade with her for a while longer. He needed to get access to the vineyard cellar and she was the best person to help him achieve that.

He had woven the lies and tales carefully so that Maria believed it was her idea to go down into the cellar on that fateful night. She had guided him through the layers of gates and security until they stood before the cube. Gunnar, knowing exactly what it was, had made quick work of weaving a fear spell over Maria. He then pushed his magic into the cube and delighted as her growing terror filled his veins with potent magic.

She died there in that cellar. Her face was frozen in an expression of abject horror. Gunnar had savored every last drop of her fear as it began what would become a long and painful path toward the school.

He had known from the beginning that he would conduct his ascension at the school. It was too perfect to turn down. With the density of students present there and Mara and Xander to humiliate, he couldn't think of a better place. The wards had proven to be quite difficult, but Xander and Mara had a specific style to their workings. He had taken his time and looked through their layers and weavings before he was finally ready.

When he had stepped onto the school grounds, Gunnar

had thought the exhaustion would leave him on the grass for the dragon to consume. It had taken him hours of agonizingly exact work to prepare for what took ten seconds. His natural weak magic had been drained very quickly and he was reminded of his father's shame in him. Gunnar had crawled into the woods and slept until almost dawn.

He had known of Turner Underwood's hidden rooms and passages. He knew that there would be places for him to hide. It was merely a matter of getting there without some student spotting him. Gunnar had been lucky and had managed to use a mix of glamors and good timing to reach the room he had since come to call home. It really couldn't have come together any better.

Now, he simply had to gradually escalate his campaign of terror, relax, and enjoy the magic that flowed into him. His body was strong enough to hold the magic he required to become a god. It was only a matter of time.

"There was another artifact stolen from Italy last year." Mara slumped down in her seat. "The onyx cube—the one that Gerald made."

Xander sat down next to Mara. "The one that converts fear into magic?" He placed his hand on hers. "I thought that was destroyed."

"No. It was hidden in a small Italian town." She sighed. "They hid the fact that it was stolen for fear of punishment."

Xander groaned. He knew there was far too much risk

in having non-magical humans watching over magical arti-facts. He had argued against it, but he didn't get a say in how things happened.

"Are they sure Gunnar took it?" He hoped that they were somehow mistaken. "Absolutely sure?"

"I'm afraid so." She took a sip of her tea. "They found traces of his magic on the woman who was killed there."

Mara squeezed her eyes closed. Another person had died at Gunnar's hands. She wondered how many lives he had taken now. How many in the name of experimentation and improvement of the magical races?

"He's using the hounds to produce fear." Her resolve hardened. "To drain our students and form magic within himself."

"Yes." Xander took another sip of his tea. "It would appear so."

CHAPTER THIRTY-THREE

"These hounds hunt down anyone with a secret, right?" Sara took a bite of her apple. "And everyone has secrets. So, we're good friends. What are your secrets?"

Everyone looked at Sara, unsure how to respond to that. Secrets were personal by their very nature.

"I'll go first." Sara threw the core of her apple in the trash. "I have the biggest crush on Professor Hodges. He's really hot. Okay, I know, he's way older than me, but still."

Evie laughed. "I think every girl in this school has a crush on Professor Hodges." She looked at William. "Don't worry, you don't have any competition."

"I really like Disney movies and music." Philip shrugged. "They're beautifully crafted and can be really fun to sing along to."

Raine tilted her head a little and looked at Philip in a new light. He was always so put together and business-like, she'd never pictured him as a Disney fan.

"I think that's cool." William shrugged. "Disney is loved by everyone for a reason."

"I cheated on a test in first grade. I knew the answers were wrong, but my then best friend convinced me that I had to cheat from this girl Lucy." Evie laughed at the memory. "I would have gotten a better grade had I not cheated."

Raine didn't really have any secrets. She told her Uncle Jerry everything, and there wasn't anything she hadn't told her friends. There had to be something, though, so she continued to think as the others shared their secrets.

Mara had gathered every teacher on the faculty to do a large ritual that would protect the students. Gunnar had grown stronger and they still hadn't been able to find him. She knew he must be using a powerful set of wards and glamors to hide as successfully as he was.

Everyone knew their purpose within the group. This wasn't the first time they had gathered to try to protect the school. The teachers all moved into their space within the circle. Lucy moved silently around the edge of the circle and placed her herbal concoction around them. Xander lit the candles in front of them and slowly, the magic began to rise from the earth.

Lucy took her position within the circle and the ritual could begin. As headmistress, Mara led the spoken part of the ritual. The words were far too familiar on her tongue. There had been many times where she had needed to protect those she cared for.

It took them almost forty minutes to weave the base of the spell through their words. Once that was done, Lucy moved around the gathered group and handed each teacher an individual incense stick. They had been tailored to the teacher's personal magical signature and strengths. Lucy once again returned to her space and Xander lit each incense stick with a flick of his wand.

Each teacher closed their eyes and pressed their magic into the incense as it rose. They guided the smoke to form a thick wall of grey haze around them. The magic intertwined throughout the smoke and formed a dense matrix of magic that covered every element and form.

Once the matrix was complete, they pushed it out around the edges of the school grounds and pulled it back to fill the boundaries of the school building. Mara saw it in her mind's eye as it crept into every corner and crevice. It was almost midnight when the last thread of magic had been pressed into place and she was satisfied that the school was as safe as they could make it.

The teachers disbanded and headed to their cottages without a word. Everyone was exhausted and in desperate need of a good night's sleep.

Xander remained behind and offered Mara his arm.

"We're doing everything we can." He patted her hand. "Gunnar will grow arrogant and we will end him."

Mara sighed and nodded. She knew that it was inevitable but having him in her school upset her.

***

Adrien sat on the edge of his bed and looked out over the grounds. He had felt the drastic shift in the magical balance around the school. The very air around them had lightened and he felt as though he could breathe easier. He allowed himself to smile and relax for the first time in a long while. The teachers had increased the protections around them. He hoped that meant he'd be able to have a good night full of restful sleep. Adrien hadn't suffered like many of his classmates, but his sleep certainly hadn't been as good as he would have liked.

He woke in the morning to Philip complaining about something. He wasn't entirely sure what, but he recognized the tone. The sun streamed through the window and Adrien realized he'd slept a peaceful, dreamless sleep. He was ready to tackle military history class, although he couldn't quite remember if he'd done the homework for it. He rolled out of bed with a groan and looked through his folder of homework. To his relief, the essay was there.

"Are you taking anyone to the dance tomorrow night?" William tried to tame his hair. "Or are you going stag?"

Adrien shrugged. He wasn't really interested in dating.

"I'm going stag or with you guys." He shrugged again. "Whatever."

"I'm with Adrien. I haven't even thought about trying to find a date." Philip emerged from the bathroom. "I assume you and Evie will make it romantic."

William blushed. "I don't know about that." He pulled out a black satin box. "I did get her a corsage, though."

Cameron looked at him. "Oh, you went for a rose?" He showed William his corsage for Raine. "I went with some… well, I can't remember what it's called, actually."

William looked at the spray of delicate yellow flowers Cameron had chosen and smiled. Raine would love it, but he was sure Evie would much prefer the pink rose he had chosen for her.

"And you didn't get me one?" Adrien put his hand to his heart. "I'm wounded."

"And I'm starving." Philip grinned and picked up his book bag. "I'll see you guys at breakfast."

"No trying to steal my pancakes," William called after him.

CHAPTER THIRTY-FOUR

Raine had taken a long time to pick out the perfect dress for the dance. The theme was winter wonderland which really limited her color options. White was the most obvious choice, but it was difficult to find dresses that didn't look like wedding dresses. She was sure that Cameron would run for the hills if he saw her in something that looked like a wedding dress. She had finally found a simple white satin dress with delicate silver roses down the bodice and a translucent silver layer over the skirt.

Her shoes were remarkably comfortable for pumps and now, she only had to tackle her hair and make-up. They had never been something she'd really focused on or studied. This time, she wanted to look beautiful for Cameron. It was their first big formal dance as an official couple.

Christie had left them with a heap of potions and lotions before she left to get ready with her junior friends. Raine looked at the labels and found they meant absolutely nothing to her. One was for sheen, another for matt or something, and she was lost. Evie sat down beside her and looked through everything.

"I learned a lot about make-up from my aunt over the summer." She picked up a silver pot. "We'll start with this."

She stroked Raine's hair gently with the silver ointment. Raine watched with a delighted smile as her hair began to sparkle like small diamonds. It wasn't too flashy, but it added a pretty edge. Evie continued to add a small dusting around her eyes that made Raine's eyes pop and finished it with a small spell to add a gentle glow to her skin. She felt as though she really looked beautiful. She stood and thanked Evie.

Sara and Evie helped each other perfect their looks. Sara had chosen a large silver dress with pearl snowflakes adorning her hair and throat. The skirt floated around her and fell to just below her knees. Sara's heels were very sparkly and Raine was sure they'd glitter under the light of the ball.

When the boys came and knocked on their door, the girls were all confident in their looks. Sara looked forward to having fun dancing with Philip and Adrien. She'd had a blast at the last dance they'd attended together. The guys had never made any moves and it was simply a night of fun and laughter. That was something Sara desperately needed.

She opened the door and stepped aside to reveal Raine and Evie. Cameron looked at Raine in her classic, simple dress. He felt like the luckiest guy at the school. She looked stunning and he couldn't believe he'd been able to convince such an incredible woman to be his girlfriend. Realizing that he stood there like a dork, Cameron pulled out his corsage and attached it to Raine's wrist. She admired it with a broad smile and he was relieved that he'd made the right decision.

"You're stunning. I'm pretty sure my jaw actually hit the ground." William took a step toward Evie. "Are you sure you want to go with me?"

Evie laughed. "I can't imagine going to the dance with a more perfect partner." She took his hand. "You look pretty hot yourself."

"Cameron found me a suit and Philip helped me tame my hair." He couldn't believe Evie had chosen him. Even after these months together, he felt like he walked on air. "Would you like my corsage?"

Evie laughed and William attached it for her. She admired it and decided it was exactly what she would have chosen for herself. He was proving to be the perfect boyfriend.

The group headed down to the ball with Sara in the lead. She had Philip and Adrien on either arm and a huge grin on her face and looked forward to dancing the night away and having a night full of laughter. A couple of junior guys paused to look at her, but Adrien glared at them. He didn't want to date Sara, but he wasn't in the mood to deal with juniors pushing their luck either. She leaned against him for a moment and continued as if nothing had happened.

They entered the dining room and saw it had truly been transformed into a winter wonderland. Snow gathered in the corners and along the edges of the room. More snow fell from the ceiling but paused above head height before it returned to the ceiling overhead to fall once more. The air was filled with the scent of fresh pine and snow. Pines seemed to have grown around the edges of the room although they were really glamors of them that had been pressed against the usually plain walls. It felt as though they had carved out a space within a large forest.

The band played familiar rock and pop music from atop a snowy platform. Everyone wore snowy colors and captured the stunning, crisp appearance of the room. Raine breathed in deeply and sighed with contentment. It was perfect. This was the night she needed.

Cameron led her over to the punch bowl, knowing that she wouldn't be ready to dance for a little while yet. He ladled a cup of silver punch for her and took one for himself. The taste of fresh peppermint and warm chocolate filled his mouth. Maybe he would simply spend the evening drinking the punch and not worry about dancing.

They sat at one of the small tables hidden under a pine tree and watched the crowds on the dance floor. Sara was at the very heart of the dancing, exactly where Raine expected her to be. She leaned against Cameron and enjoyed the music surrounding them. Evie and William were already off dancing, but she wanted to enjoy the happy buzz that filled the air for a little while longer. Everything had been fear and anxiety and it was so refreshing to have nothing but music and happiness.

Cameron's favorite song came on and he took Raine's hand and led her onto the dance floor. He put his hands on her hips and they moved to the heavy beat of the song with blissful smiles on their faces. She indulged him and remained out on the dancefloor with him for the rest of the night.

The ball was concluded with a slow dance where Raine

rested her head on Cameron's shoulder and relaxed into him. She felt so peaceful when she was in his arms. For a short while, the outside world ceased to exist. It was only them and the song from the band.

Mara and Xander remained in the shadows of the ball. The evening was for the students, not the teachers. They remained present to ensure nothing got out of hand, but they didn't make themselves known.

Xander watched the smile dance across Mara's lips and wished he had seen it more frequently. The situation with Gunnar had left her frowning and frustrated. He missed her beautiful smile and the way her eyes lit up when she was happy. Xander took Mara's hand and led her forward a few steps before he held her close and danced with her. She was stiff for the first few beats but she soon relaxed into him and enjoyed his presence.

The protections had held, and the students were safe. Mara was glad they could enjoy their dance without the worry of hounds trying to stalk them through the hallways. The students had all worked hard and they deserved their winter ball. She wouldn't admit it to Xander, but she was glad he had insisted on dancing with her.

It had been a long time since they'd danced but she enjoyed growing closer to him. He had been her anchor through all the trouble with Gunnar. They supported each other through the long sleepless nights and gave each other space when it was needed. A small part of Mara hoped they could really make it work this time.

CHAPTER THIRTY-FIVE

Raine frowned at the pair of students who walked down the hallway with long white Santa beards and bright red Santa hats.

"I have to admit, that's one of the better pranks I've seen." Sara hooked her arm around Raine's. "I heard that one year, people turned each other into walking snowmen. I'm glad I wasn't here for that one."

"Some people are turning people into Christmas elves. Complete with the ugly green outfit and the weird curly shoes." William shook his head. "I will vow vengeance if someone does that to me."

They turned a corner and saw a pair of said Christmas elves shouting at someone with reindeer horns and a bright red round nose.

"You did this to me."

"I did not. You turned me into a Rudolph which is far worse than an elf."

"You'll look like yourself in an hour but I'm stuck in this ridiculous elf appearance until I sleep."

"Just sleep through history. Everyone else does."

Professor Hudson simply shook her head. The head-mistress had concluded that because the pranks were merely aesthetic, the students were allowed to continue with them. She felt that it was good practice for them to learn how to break spells and defend themselves.

The library was full of reindeer and weird Santas. Raine was so glad that her friends didn't engage in pranks. She slipped around most of the students and went to her quiet corner where she pulled out the slender book they had taken from the teachers' library. It showed all the hidden rooms and their original purposes. Raine was sure it would help them understand where the thief was hiding.

She opened the first page and found it was written in some obscure language she didn't understand. The head librarian came over and looked over her shoulder.

"You'll need a spell to translate that." He smiled at her. "There's a spell to obscure it. You want the languages section."

The gnome knew exactly where that book had come from. He suspected that either William or Sara had been responsible for breaking into the teachers' library to get it. With that in mind, he decided not to help them too much with the translation. It would do them good to stretch their magical muscles a little and work with a new type of spell. They were clearly trying to find Gunnar, but he wasn't entirely sure if he wanted them to succeed. He was a very dangerous wizard. The students had shown themselves to be capable, but they were still students.

Raine smiled and headed into the languages section of the library. It was an area she hadn't spent much time in.

She wanted to broaden her linguistic skills, but she'd been so focused on improving her magic she hadn't had time. Most of the books she came across were how to learn new languages and the spells that facilitated that. She chewed on her bottom lip as she looked for something closer to revealing hidden languages.

William found the relevant books before Raine did. He nudged her and took them to the table where they settled in and began to read. She found that the spells were unpleasant. They required very fine and exact visualization which wasn't her strength. She had improved, but the level they required seemed beyond her abilities. Raine wouldn't give in that easily, though. She continued to read and looked for pointers on that part.

Between them, they found a spell that they were confident would work for what they needed. They crowded around the leather-bound book and tried to visualize the matrix required to unlock its words. Raine struggled to hold the layers in her mind as she spoke the words, but William came through. He found that the language spell came easily to him and wondered if perhaps that was something he should spend more time looking into.

They pulled their chairs in close and began to look through the book about the Underwood mansion. It began with a long-winded history that wasn't of any interest to any of them. Raine didn't want to know about the history of the architects who had been hired to create the mansion. Nor was she particularly interested in Underwood's choices for decor. She was there to find out about the hidden rooms and passages.

They went through every page and read every small

detail on the hidden areas in the school, only to find there was nothing of any real use to them. Raine sighed and wondered if they'd somehow used the spell incorrectly. It simply didn't make any sense to hide that book away in the professors' library.

The spell to obscure the words snapped back into place the moment they closed the book. Raine would have to redo the spell when she wanted to check if she had missed something. She didn't relish that thought but she'd handle it when it came down to it.

Leo and Joe finally took pity on the small group.

"What is it you're looking for?"

"We're trying to find the artifact thief." Raine pushed the book away. "We'd hoped that would give us full insight into the hidden spaces at the school."

"Weren't you told to leave it alone? Never mind." The head librarian held up his hand. "I can see that you're determined." He nodded. "I'm afraid you won't find what you're after in a book."

Raine leaned back in her chair and thought that through. She was used to being able to find whatever she needed in a book. Not being able to find the information there was an unpleasant and alien experience.

Mara woke with a start. The extra layer of wards and protections they had worked so hard to place around the school had just collapsed. She exhaled slowly and tried to think through the next step from there. It had taken a large group ritual to establish the protections they had.

There wasn't the time or energy to do that again. She couldn't do enough by herself, and she was sure the hounds were already back within the school halls by now.

The feeling that Gunnar controlled her school made rage boil through her. He brought harm to her students and she wanted nothing more than to bring great harm to him.

The unpleasantly familiar sound of nails clicking along the wooden floors came from the hall outside the dorm room. Raine sighed in frustration. That meant the protections the teachers had put up had fallen, which meant the artifact thief had grown in strength. He must have been incredibly powerful to break through everything the teachers had put in place.

She sat up and tried to reason through the purpose of the hounds as they paced back and forth in front of her door. A scream cut through the air and understanding dawned on her. The hounds brought about an intense feeling of fear that filled the entire school. They weren't there to poison the students with their desire to hunt down secrets, they were there to produce fear.

"He's making everyone terrified." Raine hissed to Evie.

"That makes sense. Isn't there some awful artifact that converts fear into magic?"

"That does sound like something the dark wizards would do." Sara groaned. "Can't they at least let me get some sleep?"

"No. Tired people are easier to scare and control." Raine pulled out her wand. "And we will not be controlled."

Evie held up her hand. "Raine, don't rush out there. I know you want to protect people, but we need to figure this out."

Raine paused and nodded. "We need to figure out how to find and defeat him." She looked at Evie. "Any ideas?"

"Well, if he uses the fear to add to his magic, then we need to remove his source of fear." She chewed on her bottom lip. "Or find a way to reflect the fear back onto him."

"We make him terrified?" Raine frowned. "How would that take away from his magic?"

"I thought maybe it would provide a feedback loop so he couldn't harm anyone else." Evie shrugged. "It's not perfect."

"It does give us something to work with. There has to be a spell to draw on someone's fear." She looked back and forth between Evie and Sara. "Right?"

"Yeah. There's a spell for anything if you look hard enough." Sara sat up in her bed. "Does this mean we're sneaking into the library?"

"We need to draw this guy out." Raine glared in the direction of the hallway where the hound still paced. "How do we do that?"

Evie and Sara thought for a long while. Christie still slept like the dead and Sara really envied that.

"Well, he's escalated recently, right?" Sara looked at Raine. "So maybe he's getting ready to make his big move. He's simply topping up the last of his magic."

"How can we be sure, though?" Raine dragged her

fingers through her hair and hit a tangle. "We can't hang around and hope we bump into him."

"Christmas holidays are soon. The students won't be here to feed his magic for much longer." Evie shrugged. "It's all I have."

Raine wasn't satisfied but they at least had something to investigate. She would find spells that would turn his fear against him. They would go head to head with this thief, and they would win.

CHAPTER THIRTY-SIX

Lucy gathered the herbs that her friends had been kind enough to collect for her. She needed to put them all into the potion and then transform that into a form that the dragon could and would take. Lucy began with the roots. She ground them up into a fine consistency while listening to the radio. There was a soothing sensation from the familiar action of preparing the complex potion.

She allowed her mind to wander as she went through the acts of preparing everything. The dragon was resilient and hadn't shown any negative effects from being locked in his deep sleep. Lucy was sure that he would be full of rage and would vow revenge on whoever had dared do that to him. She looked forward to seeing him take to the skies once more. They had seemed empty without his presence.

Lucy began work on the potion proper. She needed to stir the first batch of roots for exactly six minutes before she added the petals along with the first strain of her magic. Lucy was much like one of her favorite students, Evie. She had begun brewing potions at a very young age. They were something that came naturally to her and she enjoyed them because of that. The praise from her elders felt good and everything had spiraled from there.

The next stage of the potion making created a thick yellow fog that filled her cottage. Mara walked in and coughed as she tried to wave the fog away.

"Don't worry. That means it's coming together."

Mara handed Lucy a plate of sandwiches. "Tori was worried about you. She made the bread fresh just for you."

Lucy smiled. "She is far too good to us."

"I agree. We must spoil her and her fellow pixies for Christmas."

"I'm sure we'll find something suitable." Lucy stirred her potion exactly twice. "They enjoy fairy wine, I believe."

"That's very true."

"We'll all pitch in." Lucy placed her spoon back in its holder. "So that we can get them a nice selection."

"I'll speak to the others and see how much we can gather together." Mara looked at the frothing potion. "How long do you think it'll take?"

"Another two hours." Lucy bit into the first of her sandwiches. "Don't worry. Dorvu will wake a few minutes after I give him this."

A small crowd had gathered around Dorvu as Lucy walked

up with a pill almost as large as her arm. Elias had volunteered to open the dragon's mouth. He reached down and levered the massive jaw open to reveal a large tongue. He held the mouth open while Lucy placed the tablet on Dorvu's tongue. Elias reached over and stroked the dragon's throat to encourage him to swallow.

Everyone watched with bated breath and waited for the dragon to wake once more. Xander held Mara close. They had all grown close to Dorvu over the years. He knew that the dragon was strong and that Lucy was one of the best potion masters in the world.

The dragon's breathing shifted, and he opened his eyes slowly. He looked around and grinned at everyone, pleased to see so many people that he could talk to.

"Those hounds bit me," he grumbled.

"We know. You slept for a while. How do you feel?" Lucy patted his snout. "Any aches or pains?"

"No. I am starving, though."

Elias wheeled around the deer carcass that Horace had been kind enough to provide. Dorvu stood and devoured the deer in one quick bite. He shook himself and gave his wings a test flap before he took off and went to hunt for more food. Mara smiled as she watched him fly off after a small flock of pheasants.

He was back to himself without any noticeable side-effects. She really couldn't ask for a better outcome than that.

"The magic is changing. He'll make his move soon." Adrien looked up from his book. "We need to prepare."

Raine has suspected as much. They were close to Christmas break and if he intended to do something, he needed to do it soon.

"I have an idea." She pushed her notebook over toward the others. "Those runes should break his connection with the artifact."

Adrien studied them. "We can hide them with a simple glamor."

"Agreed." Cameron nodded. "The dining room is a good place for the final showdown."

"I can brew some potions we can use." Evie flipped through her notebook. "We'll need some healing potions and some attack potions."

"A magic drain one would be great." William smiled at her. "If he's really powerful, we need to reduce his magic as much as possible."

They continued to make notes on their grand plan to capture the thief. They had accepted that they couldn't find him within the school but everything Raine knew about his psychology told her he would come out. She had studied magical psychology as part of Agent Connor's mentoring. The thief fit into the type that needed the world to know everything he had done. That would mean that he needed a flashy exit, which was the perfect time for them to ambush him.

The group pulled together a plan that they felt confident with. Raine wasn't entirely sure that she held enough magic to lean on that entirely but combined with Evie's potions and the runes, they had a very good chance. She sighed softly and considered speaking to the headmistress or Agent Connor, but she wasn't sure they would listen. It seemed like a waste of energy and it would only risk them not being able to put their plan into action. Raine decided it was worth the risk.

Time to work toward a solution.

CHAPTER THIRTY-SEVEN

A shiver of fear ran down Mara's spine as she stepped out into the cool night air. The now familiar sound of the hounds and wraiths had circled her cottage for the last fifteen minutes. She had taken her time to dress and gather her potions before she chose to face them. They hadn't found a way to truly defeat them, but they had found that earth spells slowed them down and made them solid enough to drive off for a short while.

At first, there was nothing there. She looked out upon the scenic view she had enjoyed for the many years she'd been at the school. The calming sound of the stream filled the air where the animals were all fast asleep. Mara turned to return to her cottage, having concluded that the hounds and wraiths had left, when a howl cut through the air. A biting wind picked up and made the trees shiver and bend in the darkness.

Mara turned and saw an entire pack of hounds race toward her. She raised her wand and calmed her mind in preparation for a long and difficult fight. A weight formed in the pit of her stomach when it dawned on her that there would only be that many hounds and wraiths if Gunnar tried to stop her from reaching the school. He was attacking her students and blocking her access to them.

She wasted no time in considering what might be happening and instead, focused on filling the attackers with earth magic to make them physical. It was difficult to balance the earth magic with the explosive fire and light magic. She struggled to maintain everything and hold them at bay. She had no doubt that Gunnar would push them to harm her. He had always blamed her for losing his place in his coven.

The wraiths surrounded the cluster of teachers' cottages to make sure that no one could leave. Mara had never seen so many of them before. Their darkness blotted out what light came from the lamps near the cottages. Lucy Fowler emerged from her cottage with a look of rage and murderous intent on her face. She carried a large satchel and began throwing potions at the hounds. Explosions echoed all around them as her potions collided with the physical forms of the black canines.

Mara's magic wove its way through them and made them all physical enough to harm, but the two were vastly outnumbered. Every time she and Lucy cut through one or two, three or four more appeared in their place. They didn't move in close enough to bite, only enough to ensure that they couldn't go anywhere.

Lucy was halfway through her potions when Eleanor stormed out of her cottage with her wand raised and spells flying. She raced across the small gardens separating them and stood at Mara's side to give her support. Mara was beginning to tire and she was glad of the help from her old friend. Eleanor wove her spells with a vicious efficiency that helped cut through the hounds at a greater pace. Still, it wasn't enough. They crowded in close and pinned them down.

Soon, the other teachers were out in their gardens and did everything they could to drive the wave of darkness back. Elias threw potions with great vigor. He had wanted to shift into his wolf form and take them on wolf to hound, but Mara had stopped him. She couldn't bear to see him being poisoned should he get bitten. The risk was too great.

They were trapped and Mara knew her students were unprotected. She would hunt Gunnar down if he harmed so much as a single hair on any of their heads.

Xander had caught up on homework in his office. He walked down the stairs to retire to his cottage for the night when something triggered the wards around the vault. Xander ran as fast as he could down toward the heavy door. He found it hanging wide open and cursed. Someone had gotten inside, and he had no idea how. The lights were lit inside and he heard movement. They were still in there, which meant he had a good chance to subdue them.

Gunnar had already stolen the cube and he wouldn't allow someone else to take another even more dangerous artifact. They would have to work hard to overhaul the wards and glamors on the vault when this was all over. One break-in was bad but two was beyond ridiculous. The risk to the students of the school was simply too high. They needed to make sure that they were as safe as possible.

Xander raised his wand and walked with all the stealth he could muster. Movement came from the darkest corner of the vault where the truly dangerous items were hidden. A sharp clatter of metal falling against concrete echoed around the space. Xander cringed. It sounded as though someone was more than determined to get what they were after.

The wards and protections around the artifacts meant that they couldn't be moved without great skill and a significant amount of magic. Xander reached out with his own magic and didn't feel any waves of aggressive power that would come with someone trying to force an artifact free. He relaxed a little. That meant he had arrived in time.

He turned the corner with a curse on the tip of his tongue and found no one there. Cursing loudly once more, Xander turned and ran back toward the door. Someone had lured him down there with tricks. He pushed his legs to move faster. Not someone—Gunnar. He had been played. The door slammed in front of him and the light dulled to barely there. He slowed his breathing and went through the ward spells but found they did nothing. The door should have swung open to release him. He tried again. Once again, nothing happened.

Xander banged on the door in frustration and cursed. Gunnar had played him and now, he was stuck down there for who knew how long. At least none of the artifacts were sentient enough to try to harm him. The cool air wrapped around him and sent a chill down his spine. Magic slithered over his skin and Xander held onto his anger. Some of the artifacts in the vault would try to play with his mind. Such was the nature of the magic bound within them. He reflexively formed a number of mental protection spells around himself. He knew better than to try to hope that they wouldn't get to him.

Forcing himself to remain calm and focused, Xander stretched his magic in front of him and tried to feel what exactly had happened. Gunnar had managed to tweak the wards a little, enough that the spell words were effectively locked out for a few hours. If he understood what he felt correctly, Mara would be able to release him at sunrise. That meant that the intruder only needed him out of the way for a short while. He was launching his attack on the school and there was nothing Xander could do about it.

He ground his teeth and ran the layout of the vault through his mind. It had been built to house the most dangerous magical artifacts in existence. There were no back doors and no easy ways out. He was stuck there until Mara could get him out.

***

Gunnar stretched his legs and leaned back in the high-backed chair that he had enjoyed while he trapped Xander Powell. His plan had been many years in the works, but everything now came together beautifully. The teachers were all away somewhere and couldn't interfere. The students were terrified as the hounds and wraiths walked the halls freely. He would push them through the flimsy wards and runes on their dorm room doors soon. Then, the sweet fear would flood his veins and make him invincible.

The hounds and wraiths wouldn't actually harm the students. A dead student couldn't provide him with the sweet, potent fear he desired and would thus be useless to him. If they were close enough that the students thought they would bite, though, their terror would peak. That would allow him to drink in the most fear and step out in the world at his very strongest. Once he left the grounds, he would need to keep the cube with him and maintain the fear around him. That wouldn't be a problem, though. He had always thoroughly enjoyed having people scared of him.

He stood and ran his fingers over the pair of pitch-colored cubes. The first was so simple with a plain onyx construction, all except for a small blood-red engraving on the top. That was the real heart of his plans. That cube allowed him to feed on the fear and convert it into his own magic. Every taste made him stronger and more powerful. Thanks to that cube, he would be unstoppable come morning. He was so close now. There were only a few hours left before his body reached its full capacity for magic and he would be free to leave the school grounds.

The other cube was more ornate but it had allowed him to create the fear around him. He could have taken the other artifacts in the vault, but that would have made Xander and Mara far more determined to find him and bring him back. No, this way, he had been able to take his time and relish the chaos he wreaked. They had been too sidetracked by the hounds to really put in the effort to feel out his magic within their precious school.

Tonight was the night he would walk the halls freely without having to stay in the shadows. He would drink in the terror of the students and use it to make himself a god. When the sun rose, he would step out into the daylight and claim all that he was owed.

Gunnar opened the plain white door, which looked like another piece of the wall on the far side. He brushed a piece of dust from his expensive button-down shirt and stepped out into the hidden passageway. This was his moment and he wanted to be sure he looked his very best.

He strolled down the passageway and idly turned the orange flames of the torches a pale blue with a flick of his wand as he passed. He much preferred blue over orange. Perhaps he would do something with that when he was crowned as the god-king. The first thing he'd do once he returned to the world would be to remove his old group of dark magic wizards from the face of the earth. They had betrayed him and denounced him as weak and worthless. The last thing they would see would be him in all his glory.

Xander and Mara would be allowed to live so they could suffer under his rule. He had always enjoyed playing the long game and making people suffer. They were no exception. They had played a critical part in him losing his mentor and his place within his coven. His family had been the first to bring shifters into existence. They were a proud and powerful bloodline. It wasn't his fault that his magic had bloomed later than usual.

He would make his family kneel before him and worship him as was his right. They had taunted him and told the world he was worthless and not good enough to bear their name. Gunnar would make sure that they saw exactly what he really was and how capable he was. His natural magic might have been weak and flimsy compared to theirs, but he would become a god.

Gunnar shook his head and ignored the memories of a dark and unpleasant childhood. None of that mattered now. Xander was safely locked in the vault and Mara and the others wouldn't be able to leave their cottages. He was free to do as he pleased. First, he would stop by the kitchen and finish off that delightful chocolate cake the pixies and the Irish-American witch had made. There was no point in taking over the world on an empty stomach, after all.

Food had been the most difficult part of staying in the school. The pixies were very careful to protect their food, and there was rarely much left. He had needed to weave complicated spells over the course of a week so that they were thoroughly hidden. That allowed him to sneak in and enjoy the small pieces that were left from the night before. The spell made the pixies forget they'd left anything at all so the food wasn't missed in the morning. He had grown tired of scraps, though, and had tweaked the spells to encourage the pixies to make the foods he desired.

He took the time to enjoy the swell of fear around him. It tasted like honey and blueberries on his tongue. The door out into the main school opened easily and revealed a hallway that few students walked. It was on the uppermost floor away from any dorms or offices. He had wandered those halls on the upper level during the quieter nights when his thoughts had become too much. That night, he took comfort in the dark-green wallpaper and the old, dark wooden banisters. He had grown oddly attached to the space that had become home over the past few months.

The first step down the old stairs was in many ways the sweetest. He could feel the fear like a thick pool around his ankles. The more he descended the stairs, the more potent it became. A large part of him wanted to wander down past the dorm rooms to really drink it in. He shook his head. No, chocolate cake first. There was the entire night ahead of him to torment the students and revel in that sweet fear.

He planned to enjoy the chocolate cake while the hounds and wraiths moved into the dorm rooms. Then, he would help himself to the books that he wanted from within the professors' library. He was sure there would be important tomes in there that would serve him well during his reign. Finally, he would take his time and wander the halls around the dorms and relish the fear that resided there. This was his night, and nothing would ruin that for him.

Gunnar didn't really pay attention to his surroundings. He was far too focused on the sensations of his magic as it ebbed and flowed through his veins and the waves of honey and blueberries that coated his tongue. Nothing would dare try to harm him, not on that night.

Oh, how wrong he was.

"Something happened." Adrien peered out of the window. "There's a huge swell of magic around the teachers' cottages."

"He's making his move." Raine looked at her group. "Tonight is the night. Do we have everything we need?"

Evie went into their room, dragged two large boxes of potions from under her bed, and returned with them.

They had prepared for this night for the last week. Evie had taken every spare moment to brew her potions. Raine had studied new spells and refined those she had already learned with Professor Powell. Adrien had been a great help with that and he had also taught Cameron how to handle a blade should he need to. The shifter had taken to it well. He still preferred to fight with tooth and claw, but he appreciated the elf's help.

"Green is for health, orange is fire, black is for Adrien's blades, and white is a magic drain potion." Evie handed the potions out to everyone. They each carried satchels ready for exactly this. "Be careful with the magic drain and health ones. Don't throw the health ones at the thief by accident."

"Noted." Cameron rolled an orange vial around his hand. He enjoyed the fact he was more useful in a magic fight now that he had the potions. "Anything else I need to know? I don't normally throw these around."

"Try to make sure you're at least six feet away when you throw them. There's a risk of splash-back catching you if you're closer." Evie put the last of the potions into her satchel. "The black potion sharpens Adrien's blades."

The elf applied the thick black potion carefully down

the edge of his favorite sword. The thief wouldn't know what had hit him. Raine had been sure that he prepared for his big finale and she'd been right.

Raine felt a swell of pride as she looked at her group of friends. They'd come far together, and now, they would save the school. Her magic still wasn't as strong as the others, but she'd worked hard and she had her martial arts training to back her up. Adrien handed her a pair of long daggers with a smile. She tucked them into sheathes Sara had made for her.

She didn't believe in only having one backup plan. If their main spells didn't work or they ran out of potions before they defeated him, then she wanted to be sure they could use brute force. It wasn't ideal, but she wouldn't allow him to step outside of the school. They would do whatever it took to keep their fellow students safe.

"Should someone give a rousing speech?" Philip grinned and adjusted his satchel. "I vote not me. I'm bad at that stuff."

"Tonight, we go into battle." Cameron looked at his friends. "Our enemy may be stronger, but we have each other. Together, the pack can take down any foe, and we are no exception."

Raine leaned in and kissed him as a thrill of excitement ran through her. She turned and looked at her friends. "Are we ready?"

Everyone nodded. They had the plan arranged and each one knew their role. Raine opened the door and was not surprised to see Librarian Decker and Joe standing there with their own satchels of potions at the ready. She had suspected that the gnomes had kept a close eye on them during their preparations. Raine hadn't said anything in case she had been wrong. They had proven themselves to be strong allies, and she wouldn't turn down their help if they offered it. The gnomes were powerful and skilled magic users. The group would need every edge they could get.

"You didn't think you were doing this without us did you?" The head librarian grinned. "Where do you want us?"

Raine had already allowed a place for them while she made the plans.

"We'll funnel him into the dining room." She paused for a moment. "Can you take the bottom of the main staircase and drive him down that hallway?"

They both nodded. They were pleased to be given a key part of the plan. The gnomes were protective over the students and they would have pushed to be in a stronger position had Raine tried to hide them away somewhere. But they could watch over the group in that position at the bottom of the stairs.

"Consider it done." They turned away. "We're proud to stand at your side. All of you."

He meant what he had said. The group were fine fighters and he was more than happy to fight with them. He wished that it wasn't necessary but thinking such things was a waste of energy. Instead, he focused on the fight ahead of them. They would remove Gunnar from the school and make sure he never touched magic again.

The gnomes disappeared into the thick darkness that had consumed the hallway. Gunnar really tried to increase the fear. The hounds and wraiths hid within the shadows, but the darkness itself kept the students in their rooms.

They were too scared to try to leave, and their overall fear levels escalated. It was the perfect situation for Gunnar. An electricity ran through the air. Even Raine could sense the fear of the students hidden in their dorm rooms. Wraiths could be heard clawing at doors and hounds bayed.

The students had been given strict instructions to remain in their rooms after lights-out. That hadn't stopped the guys from joining Raine and the other girls in their room. They were too sure that something would happen to worry about the rules. Cameron wouldn't be separated from Raine on that important night. Nothing would have been able to stop him from reaching her. Someone had locked them in, but whoever they were hadn't counted on William's lockpicking skills. Evie handed everyone a potion that would allow them to see through the darkness without the need for light or fire spells. They didn't want the thief to know they were coming.

Elderflower coated Raine's tongue but her vision cleared. Everything looked as bright and clear as if it were a sunny day. She smiled and led her friends through the darkness and into battle.

CHAPTER THIRTY-NINE

Gunnar paused on the second floor of the school where he surveyed the beginnings of his new kingdom. He stood at the top of his stairs and smiled. The dorms weren't too far away, and his hounds did their job beautifully. He heard the click of their nails and their bays. When he licked his lips, he savored the flavor of blueberries on his tongue as he took the first step down the stairs.

Suddenly, everything tilted and changed. His heart hammered against his ribs when he saw that the entire floor behind him crawled with spiders—large black spiders with hundreds of beady eyes and sharp pincers ready to bite into his flesh. Breathing became difficult and his lungs wouldn't fill with oxygen. He gripped the banister while he tried to convince his body to move.

Something snapped within him and he took the first step down the stairs. Then the next. His eyes were wide with terror and sweat dripped from his face. When he took the next step, his senses started to return, and he felt the edges of the illusion. Some of the students tried to fight him. He screamed with rage and drew his wand, looking for them.

Sara and Philip were in the first position. Their job was to push the thief down the first set of stairs onto the first floor. There, the librarians would take over and drive him into the dining room where the entire group would surround him. They knew that the thief was powerful, and they'd need every trick and spell they had to defeat him.

Their fear spell had worked beautifully at first. They had turned what they could access of the artifact's magic against the thief and attacked his mind. It made him see what he was most afraid of. Sara had felt that they had a real chance when terror wracked him and forced him to begin down the stairs. Then, he tore their illusion apart.

Raine and Cameron were on the landing between that staircase and the main staircase where the gnomes waited. A small silver knife flew forward and sliced through the thief's ear. Blood trickled down his neck and he spun in search of the person who dared to throw it. Raine hid within the shadow he had created and used it against him. Cameron itched to sink his teeth and claws into him, but he wouldn't risk his friends.

The group had tried to find a spell that would allow them to communicate but they hadn't succeeded. The gnomes didn't know of anything either. That meant they were effectively cut off with only their partner at their side. Sara and Philip watched as the thief looked slowly around him and began to whisper while he looked where they thought Raine was. They each retrieved an orange potion and threw it at him. Sara's went a little wide, collided with the banister, and erupted in an explosion of heat and light. Philip's hit the thief's feet and the fire encircled him and made him scream with rage.

The thief pointed his wand at the fire and spoke in sharp, vicious tones while Sara and Philip threw more fire potions at him to force him to move down the stairs. He put the fires out almost as quickly as they created them.

"You keep throwing the potions. You have a better aim." Sara raised her hands in front of her. "I'll try the grenade spell Professor Powell taught us."

There was something about the spell Sara formed in her mind that worked beautifully with her kitsune magic. She pulled a handful of berries and acorns out of a pocket in her satchel. Her magic rushed down her arms and she pressed it into the small round objects. They floated above her satchel and she sent them hurtling toward the thief with an elegant flick of her wrist. The small missiles exploded with great bursts of light and sound loud enough that her ears rang.

Gunnar found himself pelted with pain and agonizing sound. He moved down the stairs to escape the onslaught and look for a stronger position to fight from. The moment he stepped foot on the landing at the base of the stairs, the grenades turned into sharp knives that sliced through the edges of his arms and legs. Warm blood trickled down his skin and ruined his pretty clothes. He was livid as he had spent months picking out the perfect outfit.

He stood tall and proud in the middle of the landing and formed a strong shield around himself to give him room to think. He hated resorting to shields as he felt they were an admission of weakness, but he was surrounded and his ears rang. The hounds and wraiths were nearby but the steady trickle of fear had dimmed. His magic had already weakened and those who dared to attack him were entirely fearless.

Raine held her hand up to Cameron. She didn't want to waste any magic attacking his shield. The shifter handed her one of the green potion bottles. Raine drank it and relished the zing of lime as she felt her magic and spirits rise. The thief stood in the middle of the landing with a thoughtful expression on his face. Raine waited with decreasing patience. Every moment he remained there was a moment more in which his magic regained strength. They needed to make him move again.

"We should work together and break that shield." Sara nodded at the thief. "Raine and Cameron will see it. They can continue the attack and force him to move."

Philip nodded and calmed his mind. Shield-breaking wasn't his strength, but the stakes were too high to worry about that now. Sara took his hand to offer him support as she used her magic to direct it at the thief's shield and pictured it shattering into tiny shards. Philip's warm, comforting magic wrapped around hers and it struck the shield with enough force to knock him off balance.

The shield weakened but didn't break. It was enough, though. Cameron threw a magic drain potion. Years of playing football with his pack paid off. The potion hit the weak point and the shield slipped away without a sound. The thief hadn't been touched by the potion, but he was vulnerable once more. Cameron threw another magic drain potion, but the man saw it coming and exploded the vial safely over the stairs. The shifter snarled in frustration.

Sara and Philip resumed their fire onslaught. Philip threw potions and Sara pushed her magic into them as they landed to make the fire crest higher and burn hotter. The thief fought to extinguish them again but eventually, he stepped down onto the staircase. Philip changed tactics and wove the spell Professor Powell had taught them to form throwing knives from the ether. His aim wasn't perfect, but it was enough to enrage their quarry.

Gunnar opened his arms wide and sent a wide wave of shadow toward Sara and Philip. They dropped to the ground and allowed it to wash over them like cold oil. Sara felt it press against her and threaten to suffocate her. She took deep, calming breaths and called upon her magic to send a light spell down toward the thief to blind him.

"Light," Sara whispered into Philip's ear.

He gave an almost imperceptible nod and they both formed the spell in their mind. They drove it down at the thief and blinded him with a brilliant white flash that made him stumble down several steps. They had made real progress. Raine and Cameron followed it up with a light spell of their own. The thief shouted and threw out more shadow, but his balance was already thrown off and he fell down the final few steps.

Cameron's instincts screamed at him to leap on the fallen thief and tear him apart. He remained entirely still and watched intently as the intruder righted himself before he shouted a string of vicious, deadly curses at where he thought Sara and Philip were. Cameron hoped desperately that his friends were okay.

Sara and Philip had hidden behind the banister at the side of the stairs and were glad of it. Large holes were torn out of the wall near them where the curses struck. Sara only recognized one of them and she knew it was designed to explode the recipient's heart within their chest. That only served to enrage her. How many people had he killed with that awful curse? She curled her hand into a fist but remained still so she didn't give their position away.

Gunnar needed to breathe and pull more magic from the fear around him. The sustained magical attacks had begun to take their toll. His father's voice echoed in his mind and taunted him for being weak.

His rage flared and his magic surged with it to give him enough to pull on the artifact and draw the magic from the fear deep inside him. He grinned, a savage, predatory expression, before he pushed out a fear spell in a thick wave. He felt it strike the students that dared move against him before he strolled casually down the next set of stairs.

Raine's throat constricted. The world spun around her and she felt as though she were hundreds of feet up in the sky and standing on something barely as big as her feet. Closing her eyes, she focused on the feel of Cameron's fingers entwined with hers. It was a spell. She was safe and would not lose this battle thanks to a single spell.

Cameron squeezed her hand. He fought against his terror of needles. All he could see was a comically large syringe bearing down on him. Raine whispered the breaker spell that Professor Powell had taught them. Her magic flowed as freely as a summer breeze and cut through the spell that surrounded them. She could breathe again. Cameron leaned against her and buried his face in her neck to use her scent and presence to help him regain control.

Sara's heart thudded in her chest. A giant anaconda tried to wrap itself around her waist but she repeated a chant that it was only a spell over and over. Her magic was locked deep inside her like a lump of coal. The more she tried to draw it out, the harder it locked down around itself. She reached out and pressed her fingertips to the cool scales of the large black snake.

They were surprisingly smooth. The head of the snake reared up and it looked into her eyes as its forked tongue flicked back and forth. A sense of calm filled Sara. It didn't matter if it was real or a spell. She would be okay. Suddenly, her magic pooled in the palm of her hand and she threw out the breaker spell in a wide arc all around them. Philip gasped and found he could breathe real air again.

Sara pulled him close and held him while he brushed away his tears and focused on the air around him. There was no more icy water. Only nice clean air that filled his lungs.

Gunnar felt sure that he had removed what little threat there was and stepped down into the main lobby of the school. He looked around casually and decided how he would change the decor. He preferred the sleek, modern look over the more traditional artistic look. He felt as though he would strip out all the color and make the walls a pure snow white.

Sharp pain cut through his thoughts and he saw a large dagger in his calf. He ripped it out and looked around to see who dared to hurt him. Hounds and wraiths appeared from the shadows and circled around him, waiting for his command. He had grown tired of pesky little students ruining his big night.

Leo stepped out of the shadows. He'd looked forward to a real fight. He palmed a confusion potion from his satchel and grinned at Gunnar, whom he recognized. At one point, his face had been plastered all over the magical newspapers. The story had gone that he had once been a powerful dark wizard, but he had fallen. His natural magic was weak, and his father had disowned him in shame.

Xander and Mara had disbanded the coven he had pulled together and left him weak and alone with nowhere to turn. Somehow, he managed to flee to Europe and was forgotten. Leo threw the potion directly at Gunnar's face and frowned as it bounced off a strong shield. The gnome had hoped that the attacks thus far had weakened his grip on the artifact's magic. No matter, he had plenty left in his arsenal yet.

Joe started his onslaught with the same grenade spell Sara had used earlier. He pulled out a handful of gravel and pushed his magic into it. The tiny stones pelted Gunnar's shield in a barrage of explosions and bright lights. The shield began to waver, but Gunnar hadn't given in yet.

His rage fueled his magic and pushed him into using dangerous curses that would rip through the gnome's bodies if they hit their target. Leo rolled to the side and threw a fire potion at the thief before he moved once more. Joe kept moving and throwing a continuous flow of fireballs at their adversary.

Slowly, they wore his shield down and it burst around him and left him vulnerable. The students ran down the stairs and wove the confusion spell Professor Powell had taught them. Combining their magic with the gnomes', they formed a brilliantly colored kaleidoscope around Gunnar. It twisted and spun constantly and the movement threw him off balance and prevented him from being able to think clearly.

He closed his eyes, but they wove mind attacking spells and pushed them into his inner eye too. Slowly, they nudged him down the hallway with more grenades and smaller explosions. They knew they wouldn't be able to finish him entirely until they had him in the dining room. There, Adrien, Evie, and William waited with the runes that would strip away his contact with the artifact and weaken him.

Raine and her friends had slowed down. Their magic had depleted and their physical bodies with it. They each took turns to drink a green potion, but it didn't restore them to full health. The gnomes picked up the slack and maintained the confusion spell and pushed Gunnar down the hallway until finally he stepped over the threshold and they could begin their final battle.

Adrien started the next attacks on Gunnar. He, Evie, and William were still fresh. They had eagerly anticipated his entrance. The runes flared around the room and cast a pale blue light that highlighted the hounds and wraiths that had surged in after their master. William groaned and called his Ifrit fire. He'd really hoped they'd be able to keep the hounds out of the fray.

He and Evie worked together against the hounds and wraiths and gave their friends room to go after Gunnar himself. William pushed his fire deep into the heart of the beings and Evie used some nature magic to drag them entirely into the physical world, so they went up like a flare.

They stood beside each other with expressions of deep focus and determination etched on their faces. For every hound or wraith they eliminated in a plume of smoke, there were two more right behind them. Evie dug deep and reached into her magic for more as she tried to move more quickly. Her friends struggled against the thief and the gnomes were close to being overwhelmed too. They needed to turn the tide in their favor.

Gunnar turned his attention to the runes that surrounded him. They had been well carved and thrummed with thick magic, but they hadn't anticipated how powerful he would be on that night. He had prepared for his ascension to a god for a decade. A few runes wouldn't hold him back. He reached into each one and shattered them in a spectacular fashion. The fresh wave of fear from the students created a rush of ecstasy that raced through him. He felt like the god he was.

Now it was time to finish those foolish students once and for all.

He raised his hands and reached deep into the artifact magic. Fear had become his tool, and he would wield that tool like a scythe. He pulled upon the fear and pushed it outwards to drive the hounds and wraiths away. They were replaced by a mental attack that drew upon the deepest, darkest fears of every being present within the school boundaries. Terror filled the air and he reveled in the sensation.

Raine's chest constricted as she suddenly stood upon a tiny platform far above the city. The buildings were tiny pinpricks below her and the birds wheeled around her in mockery. Her lungs wouldn't fill with air and her hands trembled. If she moved even a small fraction, she would fall to her doom. It would take minutes to fall that far. There would be plenty of time for the fear to consume her.

Philip fell to the floor and felt the water rush down his throat. He looked desperately around him to find an escape. He was deep below the surface. Darkness crept slowly around his vision while his lungs filled with water. His body didn't respond to his wishes. Try as hard as he might, he couldn't swim to the surface.

Sara froze in place as hundreds of large snakes in every shape and color surrounded her. A cobra stretched up and hissed at her and its hood widened as it stared into her eyes. Her heart threatened to explode in her chest. Her mouth had gone drier than the desert she now somehow sat in. There was no one to help her this time. Her friends were gone. There were only the snakes.

Leo felt the darkness hit him like a sledgehammer. His instinctual mental protection spells kicked in enough to stop the very worst of the terror from consuming him. He dug deep into his magic and focused on the solid feeling of energy that ran through his body as he felt his feet sink into the cool, wet quicksand. It would drag him down slowly. Any move he made would only make it set harder than concrete. All he had to do was stay calm.

The gnome closed his eyes and forced himself to breathe slowly. Gunnar now attacked them on an unprecedented level. They needed to push back, and he knew the perfect spell to do that. First, he had to get himself out of the terror-inducing cage the wizard had formed around him. The gnome ran through every spell-breaking spell he knew. Finally, he settled on one that would be strong enough to get him and whoever was closest to him out. Once he had an ally, they would be able to free the rest of the group.

Tori and the other pixies rushed from the kitchen to see what was going on. Suddenly, they were surrounded by flames. Tori felt the heat press against her skin and drive her backward. She had never known fear like that before. Her magic remained buried deep within her and left her trapped and alone. She swallowed hard and tried to reach for a water spell. Something. Anything to get her out of there.

Gunnar enjoyed the pixies' fear the most. It came with an extra touch of vanilla that he particularly enjoyed. He looked around the dining room where the group who had dared to go against him were all curled on the floor and trembled in terror. As much as he wanted to stay and watch them be slowly devoured by their own phobias, he was hungry. That chocolate cake called to him.

Outside the dining room, the air was filled with the sweet sounds of screams and cries of anguish and absolute terror. Every single student in the school had been struck by Gunnar's fear spell and that magic filled him. He almost fizzed with magic. It ran through his veins and gave him a feeling of complete invincibility.

Leo peeled the fear spell away carefully so Gunnar wouldn't know what he had done. The spell threaded out to Raine who was closest to him. She gasped and her eyes flew open as she was suddenly freed. She pressed her palms onto the solid floor of the dining room and took long, deep breaths. Finally, she was back on solid ground.

The gnome moved over to her and helped her to stand. Speaking in a hushed whisper, he pointed to the others.

"We'll free them but need to do it in a way that will ensure Gunnar doesn't know we've done it." He looked at Raine whose face contorted with fury over what had been done to her friends. "We'll start with Joe as he'll be best able to help us with the others."

Raine nodded and listened to the gnome's instructions for the spell. It was deceptively simple but required absolute focus. She kneeled beside Joe with Leo and whispered the words with him. Her magic sank into the tight bonds wrapped around the librarian and teased them away from him to allow him to breathe again. Slowly, they peeled the spell back and Joe opened his eyes.

They moved through the group and released everyone as quickly as possible. Raine hugged Cameron tightly and kissed behind his ear and held him until he stopped trembling. She didn't ask what he had seen. It wasn't fair to ask him to relive that.

The head librarian held up his hand when William's hands and hair turned to pure fire when he saw the state Evie was in.

"There is a spell we can use to defeat Gunnar." He

looked at each member of the group. "We must link our magic. That will allow us to take on each other's fears. We will see things that do not scare us at all and thus protect our friends and cut off the flow of fear magic."

The gnome guided the group to stand in a circle and hold hands, then led them through the spell. He watched Cameron as the shifter had his shifter magic tugged and pulled at. It was more difficult for them, but Cameron stood strong and held tightly onto Raine and William.

Once the spell was complete, each of them felt something within them, a small chain link. Cameron's lips curled back, and he snarled when he heard the screams of terror from upstairs.

"We need to protect them too." He stared hard at the gnome. "They cannot suffer."

Leo looked toward the kitchen where Gunnar had gone. The longer he remained in control, the more chance he had to escape out into the world.

"Quickly." The gnome held his hands out. "We must do this now."

The spell took an odd turn as he was about to finish it. Rather than links forming in every student in the school, the magic began to flow into Raine. He watched as she became a kind of anti-fear avatar for everyone within the building and pulled their fear away while she gained energy. Her eyes took on a soft, lilac glow and she stood stronger. The librarian smiled. The spell had chosen her because of her fearless protection of her friends.

"What happened to Raine?" Cameron looked suspiciously at his girlfriend. "Is she okay?"

"I'm great." Raine squeezed Cameron's hand. "I'm ready to end this."

She could feel the mixture of fear and strength swirl within her. It felt like a thunderstorm rumbled in her chest and her magic rippled through her hands. Somehow, she had taken on the strengths and fearlessness of everyone in the school. She was the walking antithesis of Gunnar's fear magic. He wouldn't hurt anyone again.

The head librarian made the rest of the students take a green potion before they followed Raine out of the dining room. He wasn't sure how long her body would be able to maintain that level of magic. She would need her friends around her regardless of how she felt.

Raine faced the kitchen. She could feel fear roll off him. It wasn't his own, but he grew weaker with every step. The last drip of fear had already hit his tongue and his body burned through the stolen magic. She knew that he would be reckless and desperate, which was the perfect time to take him down.

Gunnar emerged from the kitchen and stood in the middle of the dining hall. He knew something had gone wrong, but he wasn't entirely sure what. His own naturally weak magic had returned and whittled away the bliss that he had felt. The moon rose over the grounds and he was losing his grasp on the hounds and wraiths too. Someone, or something, had blocked his access to the fear. Without that, he would be nothing.

Raine walked across the room with her wand raised. She didn't know any of the vicious curses Professor Powell had warned them about. Her father's voice whispered in the back of her mind and told her to subdue him and allow

Agent Connor to handle him. She wasn't a murderer. The agency would handle his punishment, as was their job.

She began with a simple circle of fire to contain him. They didn't know how strong he would be without his ability to draw on the fear. To her dismay, he quashed the fire and turned to face her. His lips pulled back in a savage expression as he screamed the words of a deadly curse. Raine threw up a shield and rolled to the side. The curse hit the floor behind her and left a large hole in its wake.

The magic running through her veins gave her protection from his fear but she wouldn't survive a curse like that. Fortunately, her friends were right behind her. Cameron had shifted into his wolf form. He'd run out of potions and grown tired of feeling weaker than those around him. He circled behind Gunnar, ready to sink his teeth into the wizard's leg. Evie pulled on every scrap of earth and herbal magic she had ever learned. Sara and William leaned on their fire, and Philip had borrowed a sharpened sword from Adrien.

The gnomes moved to stand on either side of Raine as her support and guidance. Together, they could take on anything.

Gunnar flicked his wand and began to launch a volley of curses at everyone who so much as thought about moving. Raine and the gnomes remained in motion while they attacked with their own spells. She focused on concussive spells with bright flashes of light and loud sounds that would help confuse him. The gnomes attacked his mind directly, but Gunnar still had enough magic to be able to hold them off.

Adrien, Philip, and Cameron edged in closer with plans

to attack his physical body. Raine saw them move out of the corner of her eye. Cameron inched forward with his body low and his focus entirely on Gunnar's upper thigh. She had never seen him hunt before, but she admired the predatory grace with which he moved and was glad to have the powerful wolf on her side.

Gunnar now grew desperate and he tried to force another fear spell onto the students. Raine felt it press against her mind. Flashes of syringes, fire, and darkness formed and faded. They weren't things that concerned her in the slightest. The strength of her fellows ran through her and allowed her to protect her friends and the student body.

Tori and the other pixies had snapped out of the terror and were absolutely livid. They buzzed into the kitchen, their wings flapping, and burst back into the dining room. Their pixie magic flooded their systems as they began to throw knives, cleavers, and shards of glass at Gunnar. They circled him and attacked him with a ferocity Raine hoped she never experienced again. His shield held but Sara and William surrounded him with an inferno of fire and Evie battered him with sharp-thorned vines and poisonous berries that exploded on contact.

Raine and the gnomes moved in closer to Gunnar as he began to falter. She would make the final blow. The spell they had woven would allow her to tear out the connection he had to the artifact and render him entirely helpless once more. She merely needed his shield to fall so she could do it.

Cameron saw a weakness in the wizard's shield and leapt forward to sink his teeth deep into his thigh. The wolf shook his head violently and ignored the beating Gunnar gave his head and shoulders. Nothing mattered but keeping his friends, his pack, safe. He dug his claws in, shook his head harder, and ignored the increasing pain as Gunnar hit harder and attempted to throw spells at him.

Philip and Adrien rushed in the moment there was a space large enough to reach their adversary. They blocked his barrage of blows against Cameron whose fur was now bloody. Adrien's instincts told him to slice the wizard's throat but no matter how hard he tried, his blades wouldn't penetrate his skin. He still had enough magic wound around him to protect him.

Joe and Leo switched gears and launched a huge spell-breaker which shattered the shield. Raine saw her opportunity, raced forward, and grabbed Gunnar's wrist. The magic within her reacted and clawed its way through his thick protections until it found the threads that tied him to the artifact. He snarled and delivered a heavy blow to her cheek. She ignored both in favor of driving her magic deeper.

The threads snapped, and Gunnar dropped to his knees, sobbing. Raine rushed to Cameron and wrapped her arms around his shoulders to bury her face in his bloody fur. He licked her face and she pulled away enough to allow him to shift. He touched her cheek tenderly. His fingers came away bloody.

The gnomes had bound Gunnar in thick black ropes and included a gag. The head librarian now tried to talk Tori out of slicing him into small pieces for daring to hurt her students.

"The best thing you can do for the students now is

make them good food to lift their spirits." He lifted his hands placatingly. "I promise you it will help."

Tori finally relented.

Raine felt the spell leave her and she slumped against Cameron, suddenly exhausted. As much as she wanted to crawl into bed and sleep for two days, she knew the night wasn't over yet.

CHAPTER FORTY

"We need to destroy those artifacts!" Raine pushed to her feet. "No one can suffer like this again."

She glared at Gunnar who still sobbed.

"Where are they?" She trapped his chin in her fingers and made him look at her while she removed the gag with her other hand. "Where are the artifacts?"

"You'll never find them." He laughed maniacally. "Never, never."

Raine rolled her eyes. "Librarian Decker, is it possible to use a spell and follow Gunnar's magical trail?"

"It is." The gnome walked over to Gunnar and plucked some hairs from his head. "I'll need some supplies from my office."

Raine took the time to study her friends and make sure that everyone was okay. Evie hugged her tightly and stroked her cheek gently. She retrieved a yellow salve from her satchel and applied it to Raine's cheek.

"It'll reduce the pain and help it heal quicker." She hugged her again. "You were incredible."

"I couldn't have done it without all of you." Raine looked at everyone. "We all played our part. None of this would have come together without you."

Tori came out of the kitchen with a plate piled high with brownies. Raine breathed deeply and her mouth began to water at the rich, decadent chocolate smell.

"They smell divine." She grinned. "Thank you so much, Tori. You're such an incredible part of this school and we're so lucky to have you and your friends."

"These are packed with healing herbs. You'll still have a bruise and some tiredness, but they'll make you feel much better." Tori held the plate out to Raine. "Take two or three."

Raine realized she was ravenous. Her stomach growled, and she picked up three brownies eagerly before Tori offered them to Cameron. She bit into a brownie and found it to be the perfect mix of gooey and chewy. The flavors exploded on her tongue and she closed her eyes in bliss. Cameron put his arm around her waist and they enjoyed their treats in quiet peace.

Evie went to the others and made sure they didn't have any injuries that might need some healing salve. Joe smiled as he watched the little healer do her thing. She had mentioned thinking about becoming a baker, but he knew that she was a healer at heart. Raine and her friends had proven once again that they were strong and capable. The school was lucky to have them watching over it.

Xander had run through every possible spell he could

think of to open that vault door. He knew that shouting and screaming would only make his throat hurt as no one could hear him. Irritated, he leaned against the wall and thought through the catalog of artifacts in there with him. Could there be something he could use?

The shadow of his dark magic rose, and he closed his eyes. No. He was not willing to take that risk. Dark magic was behind him. He would wait until Mara realized he was gone. The days of thinking he could use dark magic and remain one of the good people were long gone. He had learned that lesson and had no intention to slide down that slope again.

With that in mind, he moved to the corner near the door and settled himself into peaceful meditation. He knew that while Gunnar had trapped him in there the school would never fall. Even if the wizard had managed to capture Mara, the students were far too dedicated to allow him to last until the sunrise. He and the other teachers had taught them well. They were the future guardians and protectors.

***

Mara's chest heaved as she continued to weave spells against the constant waves of hounds and wraiths. Lucy had run out of potions an hour before and slung spells along with the rest of them. Agent Connor had tried to help but there was nothing he could do but throw potions with Lucy.

The school was so close and yet it felt so far away. Mara wouldn't allow Gunnar to win. She would fight her way through his pets and save her students. She wasn't sure how she could do it, but she would not let him harm a single hair on any of her students' heads.

Suddenly, the hounds and wraiths were gone. Silence descended, and Mara looked around to find the trap. There was nothing. She raced across the grounds toward the school where her students were locked in with that madman. The other teachers were hot on her heels as they ran with everything they had across that frosted grass. All Mara could think of was how she would do whatever it took to keep them safe.

Something made her change direction. There was a problem with the vault. She couldn't quite put her finger on what it was, but she sent the others into the school and hurried to the hidden door. Max refused to leave her side and followed her. The channeling energy professor turned out to be exactly who she needed.

Gunnar had screwed up the wards on the vault and somehow, Mara knew Xander was trapped in there. Max was an expert at fixing wards that had been bent and manipulated like that. The gnome pressed the palms of his hands against the door and closed his eyes. He channeled the magic from the grounds around him and squeezed it gently into the gaps of the wards. Slowly, he expanded it until they gave way and the door could be opened.

Xander burst out with his wand raised. He relaxed and grinned when he saw who stood there waiting for him.

"Gunnar has been subdued?" He looked from one to the other. "It's over?"

"We don't know yet." Mara turned toward the main school. "Let's go and make sure our students are safe."

The head librarian ran back into the dining hall with a bright pink and yellow orb that bounced behind him.

"The tracker spell is up and running. Come on!" He waved at the students. "Quickly, before something else goes wrong."

Raine and her friends ran after the gnome who followed the orb up the stairs. Sara panted at the top.

"I really need to take up running or something." She paused for a moment to catch her breath. "This saving people thing always seems to include running."

"I'll ask the next bad guy to stay still." Adrien grinned at her. "I can't promise they'll listen, though."

The orb bounced persistently against a piece of wall on the third floor. The gnome frowned and searched for the button or something to press to give them access to the passageway that was clearly there. Cameron stepped forward and ran his fingertips over the slight indentation.

"Shifter instincts have some uses." He smiled and pulled the door open. "After you."

The orb rocketed inside and raced down a passageway lined with blue-flamed torches. Sara groaned as they began to run again, this time down the passageway. They all crowded into a generously sized room that contained old-fashioned furniture. Gunnar had filled the small wardrobe with expensive clothing, including a couple of very smart suits. Raine shook her head. She couldn't imagine what had been going through his head with that.

The pair of black cubes sat on an ornate table waiting to be destroyed. The head librarian held up his hand to tell the students to stay back while he looked more closely look at the artifacts. He knew what they were at an academic level, but they needed to understand the magic to be able to destroy them. He didn't care what Mara and Xander said. Those cubes had no reason to continue existing.

Raine wandered around the room and looked casually for any other dangerous artifacts that might have been present. Gunnar had kept the room pristine. Everything had a place and his clothes hung neatly or were carefully folded. Even his bed was made. The space didn't look like it belonged to someone who had terrorized the school.

"Gunnar was a broken man." Joe sighed. "He never found his place in the world. He searched and searched. Every time he thought he'd found it, he was rejected again. That many rejections would harm anyone."

Cameron held Raine close. He had some understanding of being rejected, but he had found his friends and Raine. He wouldn't give them up for the world. On some level, he understood how Gunnar had become as twisted as he was, but that would never excuse his actions.

"We'll need a complicated spell to break these artifacts." The gnome picked up the more ornate one. "The magic within is densely packed and comes in multiple forms."

He carried the cube to the middle of the room.

"Form a circle." He gestured at everyone present. "That will strengthen our magic and hold the magic of the cube in."

The group moved into a circle in the heart of the room.

"We'll use a complicated breaker spell. Visualize the

cube shattering from the inside out. Repeat the words after me." He lifted his hands. "Ready?"

Everyone nodded.

Once again, Raine reached deep inside herself and called upon her magic. She felt she stood a little taller since she had taken on the school's strengths. Her magic flowed easily into her wand and she formed the image in her mind. The cube was full of multiple webs of multi-colored threads. She tried to form the image of those webs snapping and the cube exploding outwards, but she struggled.

Cameron closed his eyes and formed the image in his mind. He couldn't actively use his shifter magic, but he hoped that either the gnome or Raine would be able to channel enough from him that he could help. There had been a time when his lack of ability to wield magic would have made him irritable, but now, he had his friends. He knew they each had their strengths and weaknesses, and he helped keep his friends safe.

Raine held back a sigh as she continued to struggle with the image in her mind. She refused to let her friends down. Leo spoke the words clearly and she repeated them along with everyone else in the circle. Still, her magic didn't seem to move in the way that she expected. She opened her eyes when he finished speaking and was surprised to see that the cube looked the same.

He sighed softly.

"I'm afraid there isn't enough magic between us to destroy the artifact." He smiled. "It's not your fault. You're all young and growing."

Tori and the other pixies had hung back in the main lobby and waited for the professors who burst through the main door with their wands raised, ready to defend their school. They were, instead, confronted by Tori with a large plate of brownies and a broad smile.

"What happened?" Mara looked at the holes in the walls and floor. "Is everyone okay?"

"Evie and her friends saved the day with the help of Leo and Joe." Tori held the plate out. "Does anyone need a brownie? They'll help heal any injuries you might have."

"Where are the students now?" Mara handed Agent Connor a brownie. "Is everyone safe?"

"They followed Leo's tracker spell. They intend to destroy the artifacts." Tori handed the agent a second brownie. "They're very tired. Do be gentle with them."

Xander and Mara led the professors up the stairs. They split up on the second floor. The female teachers went to the girls' dorms to check on the female students. The male teachers checked on the male dorms. Mara and Xander followed the magical trail left by Leo's tracker spell and continued to the hidden room. Xander knew that destroying the artifacts would take far more magic than the students had.

Mara was close behind him when they ran down the passageway and burst into the small, tidy room where Leo poked at the ornate cube.

"We have tried to destroy it but I'm afraid we don't have enough magic between us." He held the cube up. "Would you be so kind?"

Xander took the artifact and held it out to Mara who placed a hand on it. He knew they should have destroyed them when they first encountered them. He and Mara drove their magic into the cube and he felt it fold down onto itself until it was nothing but an inert disk.

He handed the disk to Leo who triple-checked that there was no magic left inside it. The gnome used his own magic to weave a ward on the disk to ensure that no one could ever apply magic to it again. The process was repeated with the other cube. That one sent a ripple of eerie red light out as it folded down onto itself. Once more, Leo made sure there was no magic left within it.

Satisfied that everyone was safe and the ordeal was over, Mara turned to the students in the room. She wasn't at all surprised to see the group. Still, she pursed her lips and folded her arms as she looked at Raine.

Leo stepped forward.

"These students showed incredible initiative, bravery, strength, and knowledge this evening. They fought with intelligence and fearless dedication to their fellows. Raine held the strength spell within her and acted as a guardian for the school, watching over every student present. She made sure that Gunnar wasn't too badly harmed so that Agent Connor could deal with him appropriately." The gnome folded his arms. "Yes, they broke the rules, but they did so in a way that maintained the teachings and purpose of this school."

Mara found that she couldn't argue with him. Partly because she wasn't entirely sure what had happened that evening.

"Tell me everything." She pulled a seat up and looked pointedly at Leo. "Every little detail."

CHAPTER FORTY-ONE

"You were grounded. You took a great risk in choosing to tackle Gunnar without any support from your teachers and superiors." Agent Connor tapped his fingers on the desk between him and Raine. "You should at least have told us what was going on."

"You wouldn't have listened. You would have said that I was grounded and thus shouldn't have looked into those topics." Raine leaned back in her chair, unwilling to budge on this topic. "Rather than investigate what I had found, you would have shut me down."

Agent Connor exhaled slowly. He couldn't deny that there was a strong chance she was right.

"Then we will agree to listen to each other more closely next time." He smiled stiffly. "I believe the headmistress wishes to speak to you."

Raine stood and left to go to the headmistress's office. She understood their frustration and her methods hadn't been perfect. The results, however, had been ideal. Agent Connor had put Gunnar into custody. He would go through the legal system and would be severely punished for the laws he had broken and the suffering he had caused. Raine had made sure that no one was hurt beyond the hound bites which she couldn't control.

She knocked on the headmistress's office door. Professor Powell opened it and she found her friends already gathered there.

"I understand that Agent Connor has already covered the main reasons we're upset with you," the headmistress said quietly. "We won't go over all of that again."

Raine moved to stand next to Cameron who put his arm around her waist.

"You have all demonstrated a great aptitude for both defensive and offensive magic. Combined with your determination, bravery, and sheer stubbornness, you have been responsible for saving several lives. For that, everyone is grateful." She pursed her lips. "That said, from here on out, you will communicate with us. We have seen what you are capable of and we will work harder to listen to your concerns."

"Yes, Headmistress." Raine smiled. "Thank you."

"Go and enjoy your last day at the school before you head home for the holidays." Professor Powell smiled. "I've been told that Tori is expecting you, Evie and William."

William's eyes widened a little. He hadn't spent much time in the kitchen and was a little terrified of the pixies. Evie entwined her fingers with his and led him into the kitchen. She had been dying to bake candy cane cookies with him. He looked around the space with wide eyes that Evie found adorable.

"You helped fight off a dark wizard who used fear to

give himself strength." Evie guided William over to her workspace. "You can manage a few cookies."

Tori bustled over and gave him a navy-blue apron.

"I'm sure you'll be absolutely fine, sugar plum. The recipes are nice and easy. Evie's our cookie queen." Tori gave William a kind smile. "Don't worry about anything. You're in the best of hands."

Evie showed him the candy cane cookie recipe and he relaxed a little. He'd made more complicated potions and survived. Cookies couldn't possibly be worse than real potions.

William took his time and made sure that everything was perfect. Evie stood back and watched with a bright smile. She had a more slapdash approach to baking, but she'd done it since she could walk. William, however, wanted everything to be perfect. He wanted to make Evie proud and that made her heart swell with joy.

They placed the first batch of cookies into the oven and she showed him the next recipe. He was pleased to see there were only small adjustments between flavors. That gave him a little confidence.

"You know, this is pretty fun." William grinned at Evie. "And I do love spending time with you."

"Don't they make the cutest couple?" Tori gestured at the pair. "They were made for each other. Look at the way William tries so hard for Evie."

Tori concluded that they needed to spend more time in the kitchen together. The cookies were all very fine and good, but the kitchen had a way of really bringing people together. She took a recipe for a German holiday cake to Evie.

"Why don't you make a nice Stollen bread?" She looked at them both. "It isn't too difficult, and it's a wonderful treat."

"I haven't had that since I was a little girl!" Evie was filled with excitement. "Thank you, Tori, that is the most wonderful idea."

William wasn't quite so sure. He looked at the recipe and found that it wasn't as straightforward as the cookies had been. Still, he would tackle anything if it meant he could see Evie smile. They worked through it together and she guided him every step of the way. he learned how to tell when the dough was the right texture and the impact different texture would have on the final product.

When they put the cake into the oven, William had a good feeling about it. He looked forward to sharing what they'd made with their friends.

Evie took the pretty green-and-red cloth from the plate with a flourish. She revealed the array of cookies she and William had made together to their friends. He quietly removed the cloth from the Stollen bread and showed it to them.

"Is that Stollen bread?" Adrien pointed at it. "I haven't had that in far too long."

He picked up a plate and proceeded to cut a generously sized slice.

"This is a German Christmas cake and it's divine. The sponge is light and delicate, with an almond flavor that's highlighted by the marzipan." Adrien took a bite and closed his eyes with pleasure. "They nailed it. You have to try some."

Raine hadn't seen Adrien quite so excited about food before, which was enough to encourage her to try some. She bit into it and was delighted to find it even better than described.

"Does this mean you guys will bake together more often?" Raine took another bite. "I hope so because this is amazing."

"William will spend a couple of days with me and my family over Christmas." Evie smiled at him. "I'm sure he'll be pulled into the kitchen then."

"I had a lot of fun this afternoon too. I think I'll join Evie in the kitchen here more often." He looked at her. "If you'll have me, that is."

"I would love to. So would the pixies." Evie squeezed William tightly and kissed his cheek. "I'm so glad you enjoy baking."

The group ate far too many baked goods for the rest of the evening. Adrien complained that he'd never be able to walk to their room after dinner. They didn't dare leave any food behind for fear of offending the pixies, who had made a veritable feast as the last meal of the year for everyone.

The evening ended with the group stargazing from the benches in front of the school. They sat in a comfortable silence that came from solid friendship and understanding.

Sara had planned this time. Her suitcase was fully packed and completely closed when they got up in the morning.

She had added a little piece of garland to the handle to make it a little more fitting for the season.

Christie had headed out the night before to spend a couple of days with her boyfriend before she spent Christmas in London. The space was peaceful and quiet. Raine looked out over the thick layer of snow that blanketed the grounds and smiled. It looked like a winter wonderland.

Dorvu sat next to a life-size snow dragon that some of the older students had made. The dragon looked very pleased with his snowy likeness. Raine looked forward to seeing Uncle Jerry, but she also dreaded the time away from Cameron. They had grown very fond of each other over the months spent together.

"We should get going. Mrs. Beasley will be waiting with her jitney." Sara opened the door. "We don't want her to make us walk to the train station."

The girls made their way down the stairs with their bags. The boys hurried to catch up with them and they congregated in the large lobby near the front doors. Hugs and best wishes were exchanged. They had decided to exchange Christmas gifts when they returned from the holidays. With Gunnar and everything involved with him, they simply hadn't had enough time to get each other gifts.

Cameron took Raine aside and wrapped his arms around her waist. They kissed softly and smiled.

"We'll see each other for a few days." He held her close. "And we can talk every day on the phone."

"That doesn't mean I won't miss you." She kissed behind his ear. "But I am glad we'll at least have that."

"I hope you have the most amazing Christmas."

Cameron stroked Raine's hair. "I look forward to seeing what adventures the next year holds for us."

She released him and turned to Agent Connor who had waited quietly in the doorway. It was time to head home to her uncle. She needed some rest and relaxation before she took on the next fool who tried to hurt someone nearby.

Mrs. Beasley waited patiently at the jitney when Evie and Sara approached. The jitney driver helped them with their bags before she handed them a candy cane and a Santa hat with a large grin.

"We have to get into the holiday spirit!"

The sound of Christmas songs overflowed from the bus. That was only aided by the students who sang along inside. Sara waited for Philip and Adrien while Evie got onto the bus to save them some seats.

Evie sat down and watched as the students across the aisle from her formed a pair of tiny three-inch-tall snowmen and set them up on a notebook. They proceeded to make the snowmen fight to the death. The victorious snowman yanked the other snowman's carrot from its face and strutted around the notebook holding the carrot up high.

Christmas could be brutal.

A new, addictive role-playing game infiltrates the School of Necessary Magic. The lines between real world and game world are about to blur...

Raine's story is far from over. Her adventure continues in <u>Oath of the Witch</u>

For Hire: Teachers for special school in Virginia countryside.

Must be able to handle teenagers with special abilities.

Cannot be afraid to discipline werewolves, wizards, elves and other assorted hormonal teens.

Apply at the School of Necessary Magic.

Meet the first Freshmen class!

It's been Dogapalooza around here lately. A dog addition, a chocolate binge, knee surgery, a weird comment and a two-dog breakout in the new neighborhood. In case I've never mentioned it before (which means you're not in my Facebook Group…), Leela is a pibble and Lois Lane is a large mix of Pointer and mystery dog. They have been off on their own adventures lately – enough for a short story of their own - and taking me along for a few of them.

Leela is 9 years old and was the Offspring's dog. She's the dog addition - a brown and very sweet pitbull mix with short legs and has been in our household for a few months now. Recently, she tore her ACL and had to have surgery on her back-right leg. We've been through the cone phase and are in the 'no running or jumping' phase even if she's been sprinting down the hall a few times to the front door. Yelling, 'no running' has had no effect. But I've gotten her to stop jumping. Instead she bounces on her front legs. Progress.

Lois is almost 5 – birthday in January – and last night

while I was out at a Jackie Venson show at Antone's, Lois was busy digging into two boxes of chocolate and caramel turtles I foolishly left on a counter – a gift for someone. All that remained were small bits of cardboard. Thank goodness she's such a big girl – emergency vet line said she would have had to wolf down a lot more to cause a problem and to call back if she seemed hyperactive. That would be more energetic than usual, right?

Last part was their breakout last week when someone working on the house left the garage door open. I appreciate that the girls stuck together on their run and the neighbor down the street who stopped them and held on till someone caught up to bring them home. Lois is deaf and can't hear traffic. I like to think Leela was looking out for her. She's the smarter of the two. Lois is more likely to leap into action and always ready to play. She can usually be found right by my side.

Last part is about the weird comment. Recently, I've tried an online dating site and a guy asked if I had pets. When he found out I had two dogs he said that he'd read when women have dogs it means they want to be alone. Yeah, that's why I'm on the site. Apparently, Leela and Lois are helpful at screening for me too.

Best part of having them is when I come home – every time – and I'm greeted with such enthusiasm. A lot of jumping and barking and wagging tails. That ranks up there with putting out a new book and you guys asking, "Where's the next one?" before the day is through. It's a good life. More adventures to follow.

THANK YOU for not only reading this story but these *Author Notes* as well.

(I think I've been good with always opening with "thank you." If not, I need to edit the other *Author Notes*!)

RANDOM (*sometimes*) THOUGHTS?

Dogs.

I'm not against having dogs (for other people) and I like dogs, especially playing with puppies. However, I have to admit I don't like *OWNING* dogs.

Why?

Because I've had them (and enjoyed them), and I have children. Between kids and dogs, life is incredibly busy with moments of 'WHAT THE &*#&# ???"

Like the time our new puppy scratched out a chunk of the new carpet in our new house.

I was pissed for *weeks*.

In September of 2017, we said goodbye to being full-time parents as our young men left to head to college, and our last dog Calvin went to live with the "Godmother of dogs" (seriously, my mother-in-law treats Calvin like the prince of dogs he was apparently born to be. Just ask Calvin… He will look at you with those soft eyes and that "of course I am the Prince" attitude I never understood.)

After something like twenty-five years of parenting full time (you never *stop* parenting) I am happy to be able to pick up and go anywhere without worrying. I suspect that when life slows down enough that I am in one place for the year, I might look at pets.

However, by that time will we have digital pets?

If we do, fantastic. Because digital pets don't rip up my carpet.

HOW TO MARKET FOR BOOKS YOU LOVE

We are able to support our efforts with you reading our books, and we appreciate you doing this!

If you enjoyed this or ANY book by any author, especially Indie-published, we always appreciate if you make the time to review a book, since it lets other readers who might be on the fence to take a chance on it as well.

AROUND THE WORLD IN 80 DAYS

One of the interesting (at least to me) aspects of my life is the ability to work from anywhere and at any time. In the future, I hope to re-read my own *Author Notes* and remember my life as a diary entry.

Phuket, Thailand

I'm sitting looking out of the window at the…uhhh…

One second.

Andaman Sea. (GO, GOOGLE MAPS!)

It's blue, relatively calm, and beautiful. More important to me than that are the cool mountains and trees around Phuket. For some reason, the trees going up the mountains make me think of the scenes in the Star Wars movie *Return of the Jedi* where we see the monstrous Empire landing port dominating the forest.

I think I loved those images way more than the stuff happening under the canopy.

Except the parts where they were taking down the AT-ST Walkers (you know, the little two-legged walkers that Chewbacca (one of my favorite characters) was piloting?)

I have a home being built in Cabo San Lucas, Mexico, and the water out there is ALSO beautiful.

But for a long time, I have wondered if it was the wrong place to build a house on the water. I mean, I hadn't seen oceans all over the world, so did I pick wrong? It's in a beautiful location, but...but...

But nothing.

I've now seen Bali (also very pretty) and Phuket on very nice mornings, and I have to say that I (very subjective opinion) prefer the Sea of Cortez / Pacific Ocean view that I have. These areas over here are amazing, no doubt about that.

But I am a slave to Mexican food, and where my stomach goes, so goes my heart.

FAN PRICING

If you would like to find out what LMBPN is doing and the books we will be publishing, just sign up at http://

lmbpn.com/email/. When you sign up, we notify you of books coming out for the week, any new posts of interest in the books and pop culture arena, and the fan pricing on Saturday.

Ad Aeternitatem,

Michael Anderle